SHADOW EMPIRE

BRI BLACKWOOD

BRETAGEY PRESS

Copyright © 2021 by Bri Blackwood

This is a work of fiction. Names, characters, places, and incidents either are the product of the author's imagination or are used fictitiously. Any resemblance to actual persons, living or dead, events, or locales is entirely coincidental. For more information, contact Bri Blackwood.

No part of this book may be reproduced in any form or by any electronic or mechanical means, including information storage and retrieval systems, without written permission from the author, except for the use of brief quotations in a book review.

The subject matter is not appropriate for minors. Please note this novel contains sexual situations, violence, sensitive and offensive language, and dark themes. It also has situations that are dubious and could be triggering.

First Digital Edition: July 2021

Cover Designed by Amanda Walker PA and Design

❦ Created with Vellum

NOTE FROM THE AUTHOR

Hello!

Thank you for taking the time to read this book. Shadow Empire is a dark billionaire romance. It is not recommended for minors and contains adult situations that are dubious and could be triggering. It is a standalone and the book ends with a happily ever after for our couple.

It would be helpful for you read Savage Empire, Scarred Empire, and Steel Empire before reading this book. The next book in the series is Secret Empire.

BLURB

What lurks in the shadows...

I was in the wrong place at the wrong time
   When Broderick Cross saved me from an untimely fate.
   I hated him with every fiber of my being,
   And I know he won't touch me because I'm his best friend's sister.
   Or that's what I thought.
   But even with danger knocking on my door,
   The one I need protection from is him.

PLAYLIST

Who Knew - P!nk
The Man - The Killers
Americano - Lady Gaga
How Do You Sleep? - Sam Smith
Fuck Apologies - JoJo, Wiz Khalifa
Look What You Made Me Do - Taylor Swift
War Paint - Kelly Clarkson
We're Good - Dua Lipa
Shadow of the Day - Linkin Park
Safe and Sound - Taylor Swift, The Civil Wars
Try - P!nk
On Your Side - The Veronicas

The playlist can be found on Spotify.

GRACE
A FEW YEARS AGO

If Hunter made any more fast movements, I was going to leave. Every time he jumped to someone attempting to score a touchdown, it made me feel skittish about whether he was going to hit me. Whenever he watched sports, he got like this, which could be amusing, but was also sometimes dangerous due to not knowing which limb would fling out and where it would land.

"I don't think I can take this," he said as his breathing mimicked that of someone who was hyperventilating. It didn't do me any good to be sitting next to him.

"You all right?"

I looked over Hunter's head at Broderick, who'd just joined the conversation. He was sitting on the other side of Hunter and was as amused by Hunter's antics as I was. We both shook our heads.

"Do I look okay to you?"

I understood why he was in such a state. His favorite football team was in the Super Bowl, and it was the fourth quarter of a tight game. As big of a fan as Hunter was of New York sports, I was shocked that he hadn't pulled a muscle due to his motions.

After having a minor debate with myself about doing so because I feared for my safety, I placed a hand on Hunter's shoulder. "Why don't you walk it off for a bit? Take a breather?"

"Probably won't do much good, but thanks for the advice, future Dr. McCartney."

I laughed. I'd gotten into medical school last fall and if everything panned out the way I hoped, my brother's words would be accurate. Today, however, I hoped he'd get up and give me a bit of room. I feared I'd get an arm to the face when he got this excited. "You look like you might need another beer anyway."

Hunter looked at his empty bottle before looking back at the screen and he shrugged. "I could use another. Do you guys want anything?"

"I'll take another beer as well," Broderick said.

I shook my head. "I'm okay, thanks though."

With a heavy sigh, my brother stood up and walked toward the kitchen of his spacious apartment. He'd just moved in and wanted to host a small get-together to celebrate this new cornerstone of his life. He'd taken his time moving out on his own, citing various reasons, but it was great watching him get settled into his own place.

I stretched and with it, a sliver of my stomach showed between my white T-shirt and denim jeans. With Hunter out of the room and me wanting to avoid any awkwardness with Broderick, I turned to my brother's best friend and grinned. But what greeted me in return was unexpected. I watched as his blue eyes traveled up my body before landing on my face. They flashed hot, further electrifying the color I knew they were.

This was a complete change from the amused expression that we had just shared. I refused to back down from his heated stare and a small smirk appeared on his lips. I would have thought the slight smile would have lightened the intensity of his gaze, but it didn't. What I saw in his eyes was raw, smoldering, and unadulterated heat that was swallowing me whole. Intrigue lay between us, making me briefly wonder what would happen if he made a move.

But he wouldn't.

Because I was Hunter's little sister and that was forbidden under any circumstances. We knew what type of people the Cross family were and some of the things they were involved in. Getting entangled with one of the brothers would be hell on wheels, turning the life upside down of any person they were in a relationship with.

I had plans. A future to look forward to.

Still, I stared back into his eyes, mentally daring him to make a move even while my brother was in the next room. I wanted to explore that edge of darkness that hid behind his stare as I felt goosebumps appear up and down my body. What was he doing to me? Was this all in my head?

"What did I miss?"

My brother's words broke Broderick's and my stare down and made me jump. My head twisted to face Hunter and I could feel my cheeks turning warm. The last thing I needed was for a blush to appear on my face, lighting my face up like a billboard in Times Square, giving a small glimmer of what just happened.

"Outside of a few commercials? Nothing."

Broderick spoke up for the two of us, essentially closing the door on the moment we had. Part of me was grateful, but the other part of me wondered what if?

We never spoke of the moment we shared ever again.

1
GRACE

Death was a part of my job. It wasn't something that I liked or preferred, but I understood that there was a chance that it would happen on my watch.

And it didn't get any easier.

My career as an emergency room physician brought many highs and lows, and you never knew what each shift was going to bring you.

And today was one of those lows.

Watching him take his last breath with no loved ones nearby was heart wrenching. And here I was having to tell his daughter that her father had died before she arrived. It's hard not to let it get to you.

I lost him.

Looking down at his still warm body in this hospital bed didn't help my thoughts. I had done everything I could to save him, but in the end, death had taken him. He was too young, still in his fifties. It wasn't fair.

It didn't stop the thoughts that clouded my mind as I wondered if I had been better at my job, would he have lived?

Maybe that was too much to take on my shoulders, but it couldn't be helped. I became an ER doctor to help people survive. Today, I failed.

Now, as I stood hovering over his bedside, I knew I had to prepare myself. Telling a patient's family was never easy, and his daughter was on her way here, to stand vigilant at his bedside while he recovered. But there would be no recovery. His injuries from the crash had been too severe and now I had to break the news that she was too late. He'd passed on with no one, but his medical team at his side.

A knock on the door caused my gaze to shift and I watched Dr. Anita Nepal open the door and walk into the room. A mix of emotions filled me, and I sniffled in an attempt to keep from shedding tears. I rolled my shoulders back and turned to face her.

"Grace?"

"Yes?"

"Do you need anything?"

I shook my head. I appreciated her concern, but there was nothing she could do. What was done was done, and there was nothing that could change fate.

"The patient's next of kin should be here shortly."

"I know." I paused and took a deep breath before I continued. "Did Stewart Carnaby survive?"

Dr. Nepal nodded. "Yes. And he's in stable condition. Your sharp thinking saved his life."

A rush of breath left my body as I closed my eyes. At least one person had been saved from the horrible wreck that the patients were in. But my thoughts drifted back to the family that was now missing a loved one. Someone who left this world too soon because of something that could have been prevented. The accident was presumed to be a hit-and-run, and the paramedics had raced the driver and passenger of the hit car to the hospital. And now I knew only one had survived.

With a weary sigh, I stood up and rolled my neck, preparing to take on this next challenge: having to tell someone that their loved one was no longer alive.

I steeled my feelings so that I could be strong even though I was about to break someone's heart. I walked over to the lone sink in the room and washed my hands. When I looked up in the mirror, there was no disguising the shadows that had made their home under my eyes. I was willing to admit that tonight had taken a toll on me physically as well as mentally.

With a heavy heart, I dried my hands off and turned to leave. I was about to drastically change a family's life forever.

When I left the room, I first confirmed where the next of kin was and any information that had been gathered about her. With the details in my mind, I knocked on the door and opened it before walking inside.

Kendra Lennon rushed over to me so quickly that I took a small step back involuntarily. She looked barely twenty and she was going to find out that she had to bury her father. I couldn't imagine having to bury any of my family members, let alone at her age.

"Please tell me my father is okay." When I didn't answer right away, she said, "Oh. No."

She violently shook her head for a second. "No, no, no." Tears flooded her eyes before streaming down her face.

"Kendra, the car accident was severe. He was in grave condition when he arrived, and we did everything we could to save him. I'm so sorry to say that unfortunately we weren't successful, and your father passed away."

The scream she let out when I confirmed her worst nightmare was something I don't think I've ever heard come from a human before. She walked toward me and this time I didn't move back when she threw herself into my arms.

She cried with me holding on to her as I barely held it together myself.

∽

I KNEW Dennis Lennon's death would haunt me. For how long? Who know, but more than likely, it would until the next one.

Was there something more I could have done? I closed my eyes and shook my head. I *had* done everything possible for him.

It was like this every time I lost a patient. I always wondered, what if, but even after recounting everything I did or could have done differently, I came back to the fact that it was out of my hands.

Not even the hot water from what was normally a relaxing shower could ease the weariness that was floating through my body. I knew going into this job that chances were I couldn't save everyone. Still, it didn't help contain the emotions that I felt after a loss of human life. I watched as the water swirled down the drain, much like the life of my patient leaving his eyes.

Late shifts at the hospital varied, but tonight was one of the worst nights in a while. I ran my hands across my face, hoping the motion would push the thoughts further back in my mind, and it somewhat did. Maybe watching a mindless reality television show would help?

I turned off the shower and stood still for a moment, allowing the water to drip off me. I watched as the last of the water went down the drain before opening the sliding door and grabbing my towel. Once I had dried off and thrown a robe on, I let my hair hang in damp ringlets on my shoulders. An alcoholic beverage was out of the question for me because soon the sun would be rising, but I was determined to watch at least one episode of something I'd taped on my DVR.

I glanced at my phone, which had been thrown on my couch in my haste to take a shower, and didn't see any notifications, which was not surprising given how late it was. Being able to laugh at a television show helped shake the sadness that had taken over my mind and shifted the memory I had of Kendra's face when I told her that her father had died. I could still hear her wailing. She ended up being the one to identify Dennis, and I felt guilty that she'd had to do that all by herself. When she turned in my arms and wept into my shoulder, I hadn't been able to stop the couple of tears that left my eyes either.

I turned off the television and stood up from my couch. Before I knew it, the short walk from my living room to my bedroom was mostly a blur because I didn't remember moving at all. Maybe attempting to sleep this off would do me a lot of good.

The urge to go back into the bathroom to do my nighttime routine was there, but I couldn't make my body move again. Skipping it for one night wouldn't be the end of the world.

I turned on the lamp closest to me and stared for a

moment. Normally, I didn't mind sleeping alone and craved having time to myself, but this evening was different. Having someone I was close to and trusted to talk about my feelings with would have been a beautiful thing, but I couldn't remember when I last went on a date. I refused to call my mother or brother to burden them with my problems. After all, they needed to get up in the morning and go to work, so disturbing their sleep would be selfish on my part.

I could call Dad if I knew or cared where that asshole was. The only thoughts I'd want to give him would be to give him a piece of my mind over what the hell he'd done to our family. Then again, I really didn't want to see, let alone speak to the man ever again, so it was probably best not to even imagine how that call would go.

With a heavy sigh, I walked over to my window to close my blinds and noticed that someone had parked across the street and had just turned off their headlights mere seconds earlier. I couldn't make out the exact color or make of the car from here, but I waited to see what the driver would do, more so out of curiosity and another distraction from going to bed. When the driver didn't get out of the car within a minute, I closed the blinds, leaving rest of the world where it should be: outside.

I crawled into bed, hopeful that sleep would soon overtake my body and leave all of today's troubles in the past, and that tomorrow would be a better day.

2

BRODERICK

"That's all I had. This meeting is adjourned."

I nodded at my father, secretly glad that the meeting was over. A quick glance at my watch proved that this conversation had gone on longer than planned, and I still had a lot of things that I needed to do before I left for the day. Including reviewing a set of documents that I had been waiting on for the last couple of days.

"Everything all right?"

I turned to Gage, and my eyes shifted from him to Damien, to Dad. "Yes, why wouldn't it be?"

"You've been anywhere but here for the last ninety minutes."

He was right and I knew it, and seeing Dad and Damien slightly nod, confirming his statement, was a punch to the gut. I hadn't meant to appear disinterested in the meeting, but my mind had wandered to the package I was waiting for.

"I've been listening. I have a project that's been taking over most of my thoughts that I wanted to finish." That was an understatement, but I didn't want to divulge too much of what I had planned. At least, not yet.

Dad gave me a small smile and said, "I look forward to hearing about it."

I dipped my head in acknowledgment, happy to receive some positivity from him. This was an agreement that had been in the works for a while, and I couldn't wait to unveil it.

"Damien, can you stay for a second?"

Our father's question yanked the moment that we'd just had from me, and a slight scowl covered my face. I could feel Gage's eyes burning into my flesh because I knew he knew what had just occurred. Because he too lived in Damien's shadow.

I cleared my throat and stood at the same time that Gage did.

Damien looked from our father to me. "I'll stop by your office on my way back up to mine. I have something to give you."

"Okay?" It was more of a question than anything, but Damien didn't elaborate. I quickly packed my briefcase before snatching it off the chair and walking over to the door, Gage following in my footsteps. I opened the door and turned slightly to give my older brother and father a quick wave before exiting the room.

"Does it still get to you?" Gage asked right after he closed the door behind him.

"What?"

"The fact that Damien is going to be the heir to this place?"

I shrugged, but he knew my feelings about that as this discussion had come up between us once before. It made sense that Damien would be next in line. He was the oldest and wanted the position. None of that helped sway the way I felt about the dynamics that were at play.

And Gage wasn't letting it go. "If the tables were turned, how would you feel?"

I didn't answer the question right away. Instead, I kept walking toward the elevator that would take me to my office. Thankfully, no one was around to hear the interrogation. I took a deep breath and looked at Gage. "I don't necessarily mind that Damien is going to be the head of everything here. My goal is to further establish myself outside of Cross Industries so that when the time comes and Dad retires, everything that I've worked for won't solely be attached to the family business."

The soft sound of the elevator announcing its arrival dragged my attention away from what Gage and I were talking about. We stepped into the elevator and watched the doors close before Gage spoke.

"I've been thinking the same."

"Does that explain why you've been super busy for the last few months? Are you going to your floor?"

I stepped forward and pressed the button for my floor and then glanced back at him. He nodded and I pressed the corresponding button before taking a step back.

I was fully expecting him not to answer my first question, but he said, "Sort of."

Our conversation stopped after Gage's response, as the elevator announced its arrival to my floor. "See you later," I said as the doors opened.

"Later."

I left the elevator, leaving the uncomfortable conversation

behind, with my plan was still intact and a secret. It wasn't something I wanted to reveal until I had everything set in place. If it worked out the way I planned, I would stand to earn millions in the short term and billions in the long term, which would be added to the money I already had.

I gave a polite smile to Jenna, my assistant. She was on the phone and placed it back on the receiver as I walked up to her desk. "Did any deliveries come for me?"

Jenna took a second to recall something. "Ah, yes! Sorry, things have been super busy this morning. I left it on your desk."

"Perfect," I said as I walked past her and into my office before closing the door. I could see the manila envelope sitting on my desk, begging me to open it and read its contents.

Yet I was hesitant. Could this be the big break I'd been working my entire career toward?

I checked my watch, wondering when Damien would arrive, as the file on my desk taunted me. I had a feeling that as soon as I opened it and tried to read the documents, I was going to be disturbed. Just as I sat down at my desk, my office phone rang.

"Broderick," I said. I assumed that Jenna had sent the call through for good reason.

I stroked my chin once as the person on the other line continued to drone on. Questions about whether I should have answered the phone or not were answered the longer the conversation went on. Figuring I could make better use of my time, I opened the manila envelope, and scanned the first page of the contract. When I looked at my wristwatch and noticed that he'd taken up twenty minutes of my life that I'd never get back, I knew it was time to end this call.

"Josh, I have another meeting I need to prepare for. If you can just send any documents along to my assistant, I'll be happy to go over them at my first opportunity."

"Thank you so much, Mr. Cross."

"Likewise."

I placed my phone down on the receiver once again and picked up my pen. I was determined to finish reading the contract that I removed from the manila folder, but the world was determined to not let that happen. I groaned when someone knocked on my office door. It seemed as if today I wouldn't catch a break.

"Come in," I said, not trying to hide the irritation that I felt in my voice. When the door opened, I found Damien standing on the other side. He said nothing as he closed the door, instead choosing to toss something onto my desk.

"What the hell is this?" I picked up the black object and examined it. It was a key with an intricate design, yet it was heavier than expected. The letter *E* was embossed on it in gold.

"Your key for getting into the basement of Elevate."

I raised an eyebrow at his reply. "Why am I just finding out about this new security protocol?"

Damien crossed his arms over his chest. "Because we agreed that Kingston and I would find a security solution due to the latest threats we've received related to the club. Everyone who is a member of the sex club is getting one."

He was right, he had volunteered to be the point person on the matter and agreed to come in with Gage if something needed to be discussed. But it was clear that he and Kingston had come to an agreement on this.

I flipped the key in my hand. "I like it. It's inconspicuous if someone were to actually attach it to their keyring, but also still carries an air of..."

"Sophistication?"

I pointed at Damien briefly. "Yes. That's the word I was looking for. Thanks for handling all of that."

"Don't thank me. My main objective was to protect Anais whenever we came to the club, everything else being protected just fell into place."

I chuckled. "Okay." I knew he meant every word.

"Are you going to be at the party?"

I raised an eyebrow and sat back in my chair. "Why would I miss my oldest brother's engagement party without good reason? I might look like Gage, but I assure you we are not the same."

Damien shook his head. Giving him a hard time was a highlight of my day. "Has he spoken to you?"

"Gage?"

Damien nodded.

So, he had noticed it too. "I'm not sure. I brought it up to him, but you know how he likes to brush things off."

I knew what he was talking about. Gage was tightlipped about his absences from certain events.

"Well, if you find anything, let me know."

"Will do. How is Anais?"

That caused a smile to form on Damien's face. It didn't take much to see the love that he had for his fiancée and how she'd changed him for the better.

"She's doing well. I forgot it's been a few weeks since you've seen her. Everything is great."

"I'm glad. Looking forward to the party."

"Since when do you enjoy socializing with the people Mom and Dad usually deal with? Let's be honest, a significant portion of them will be there due to their connection to them instead of to Anais and me."

"Since I'm going to have access to booze."

"You're full of shit. Especially with the stash we both know you have at your home."

I chuckled, remembering the evening Damien came to ask me for advice about Anais. "I do love to entertain."

"In more ways than one, I'm sure."

"Just because you're out of the game now because you've found love doesn't mean the rest of us are. You were just in a similar situation as me not too long ago."

"Touché. Anyway, the reason why I came down here was to give you that." He gestured to the key on my desk. "I should probably end this social call and get back to work."

I knew that was code for finishing everything he needed to do and get back to Anais as soon as possible. "Okay, I'll see you soon."

With a slight nod, Damien left as quickly as he came, and I was happy to get back to focusing on the work that was still on my desk. But Damien was right to call me out on my bullshit about going to his engagement party. Yes, I wanted to be there to support my older brother, but that wasn't the only reason and it had nothing to do with the open bar I knew Mom and Dad had planned for the big celebration.

I read through the documents on my desk, combing through the file in hopes of presenting Dad with it at the latest by tomorrow morning. As I read through the papers in front of me, anger coursed through me. This deal was bullshit, and it was clear as day that Malcolm Harris was trying to pull one over on me.

Malcolm was heavily connected to everyone in New York City to the point where I was shocked that he was still alive due to him having a hand into so many pockets, whether it be local politicians or the different Mafia families. Never had I heard of him so blatantly attempting to fuck someone over until now, all over a deal that would have given him another revenue stream. Yet the redlining of the contract that I had given him showed that he expected to get way more money than I was willing to give. He dared to try to fuck me over? As if I wouldn't review each change that he made to this document?

The buzzing of my phone didn't annoy me nearly as much because I welcomed the reprieve. This would get solved and it would get done quickly, but I wanted the distraction. A glance at my phone told me that it was a text message.

Hunter: *Yes, I'll be at the party and Grace is coming too. Already RSVP'd for both of us.*

Me: *See you there.*

I couldn't help it, but I read over her name once again as a smirk formed on my face. This might be fun.

3
GRACE

"What do you mean you can't come tonight?"

"I can't. I still have work to do at the office."

I sighed. I wasn't surprised by his answer. Hunter was trying to become a partner at his law firm, so he needed to put in longer hours. But this wasn't the evening for him to miss.

"You'll still have Broderick and Gage there."

I cut my eyes over to the phone. "I wasn't worried about anyone I knew being there, I hoped that this would be an opportunity for us to catch up." Our schedules hardly matched up other than the odd Sunday we got together to watch sports, and I'd been hoping this would be a great opportunity to hang out with him. Plus, in a way, I'd wanted this to be an evening that would take my mind off the soul that was lost yesterday. Seeing the look on his daughter's face as I told her the news nearly broke me and made me want to hug my mother tighter. I needed to call her either today or tomorrow.

"I guess our schedules will line up at some point."

"Aw, thanks, Grace. Shoot me some dates that you have available, and I'll try to match it up with mine."

I plastered on a fake smile, even though Hunter couldn't see me. "Will do."

"Thanks. Oh, and I'll send my regards to Damien, so you don't have to worry about mentioning it to them."

Hunter knew that I would have thought long and hard about an excuse for him that would probably end up being believable. "Okay. I have to go get ready."

"Talk to you later."

"Bye, Hunt."

I hung up the phone and took my time pulling myself together for tonight's event. I prepared myself for the questions I would undoubtedly get socializing with some of the people at events like this, and having Hunter there usually softened the blow. But that wouldn't be the case this evening.

I smoothed my hands down my dark green, almost black gown that I'd bought last minute. Thankfully, the seamstress altered the dress slightly so that it fit perfectly to my body. I didn't fully understand why I was going through all of this because I wasn't the guest of honor.

On second thought, it was probably because it would give people less to talk about.

I pulled at the long sleeves of the dress and the deep V that showed off my cleavage. At least the mid-thigh split would make the gown easier to walk in and give me an excuse to show off the red bottom black pumps that I never got a chance to wear. All of this would take some getting used to since I spent most of my life nowadays in scrubs.

I flipped my long, blonde hair over my shoulder, making sure that the waves that I had styled earlier were still holding before I grabbed the black clutch that I would be using tonight. With one more glance in the mirror, I walked downstairs and found that the car I had hired for the evening was already waiting for me.

The driver gave me a polite smile as he held the door open for me, and once I was situated in the back seat, he took off into the evening, allowing me some time to sit with my thoughts as I tried to mentally prepare myself for the night ahead.

I had no problem socializing with others, after all, I spoke with many people as due to my profession, but some of the people that would be at this event pitied me. What made it worse was that it was no fault of mine.

Although it was a result of my grandfather's initial embarrassment of the family, my father decided to one up him last year with what he did to Mom. I didn't know if Hunter noticed similar things when he was around these people, but I couldn't turn my brain off to ignore them. Their heated gaze as if they knew everything about me drove me out of my element, which was why I rarely attended functions such as this.

"My name is Patrick and I'll be your driver for the night. Do you want me to switch the music station?"

Patrick's words stopped my thoughts from swirling too far down any rabbit holes. I mentally thanked him before I responded, "No, this is perfect."

He'd chosen a channel that was playing light jazz, and I let the soothing sounds of the song take over my mind.

You'll still have Broderick and Gage there.

My brother's words hung around me. I knew he would more than likely be there to support his older brother, but more often than not, Gage was absent from a lot of the get-togethers that the family had. No one brought up why and I didn't ask. Then again, it was a party, so chances were that he'd be there.

But Broderick spun different feelings in me and at least I could count on him being there. Broderick and Hunter met in elementary school and had been inseparable ever since. It was almost as if he'd become another member of the Cross family, which was helpful in many ways.

The ride continued in silence, with just the soft jazz lulling me into a false sense of security. After all, I didn't know what to expect once I walked into this party.

"I'll stay in the area so give me a ring when you are ready to leave."

"Will do." I had rented the car, which I had paid a set number of hours for, in hopes of using it as an excuse to leave the party when I had enough socializing. Having the driver here was a safety net that I wasn't afraid to use.

This is only for a short period of time. I can make it through this.

After the kind driver opened the car door, he helped me out of the vehicle, and I steadied myself in hopes of not showcasing any of the nerves that were running through my body like a tornado. I almost wished one would take me away from this place right now.

No. I wasn't going to devolve back into the feelings that I had during my teen years. There was nothing their judgmental looks could do to me now.

I took a deep breath as I lifted my dress slightly to walk up the stairs to the Cross home. As soon as I walked through the door, I could feel the stares as I crossed over the threshold, and I politely nodded at one woman who was standing near the door. Then Selena Cross walked into the hallway and sent a smile my way.

"Grace! It's so nice of you to come."

I grinned back at her, happy to have a familiar face in a sea of the unknown. I talked to strangers on a regular basis, but it felt as if I was walking into a den of vipers when I walked into the room. The warmth that radiated from her helped ease some of the turmoil that was alive and well in my mind.

"I'm happy to be here. Can't believe that Damien is getting married."

I wasn't kidding. Any of the Cross men getting married was a weird thought let alone seeing it happen.

Selena leaned in closer. "Thank you for all that you did to help Anais. We wouldn't be celebrating their love on this occasion without you." She reached over and gave my hand a small squeeze.

I returned the motion before Selena glanced behind me.

"Is Hunter coming along? I swore he was on the RSVP list."

I gave her a small smile, somewhat amused that she remembered his name out of all of the names that were probably on the list. "He couldn't make it due to work and he's sorry that he is missing all of this."

Selena shook her head. "Hunter reminds me so much of my husband and sons. They work so hard that it is impossible to get them to relax and do something fun."

I nodded, clutching the words that I wanted to say. I knew for a fact that Selena's sons and sometimes my brother had plenty of time for "play" at Elevate. This wasn't the audience nor the time or place to discuss the things I had heard about their adventures. Although I had never been to Elevate, and things that happened there were supposed to stay there, not everyone could keep their mouths shut.

Selena sighed and I saw her smile drop for a second. "I should probably continue making my way around the room, but please let me know if you need anything. The couple of the evening and the twins should be in the big room just over there." Selena gestured behind her as the smile was firmly back on her face.

"Okay, I will. Thanks."

Selena moved around me and walked in the opposite direction. I straightened my shoulders and took a few steps toward the room she gestured to just moments ago, and as I walked inside, I could feel several eyes on me. Once again, it was as if I had entered a fishbowl. It was almost as if I could hear their thoughts circling around my family and what we had done to deserve what we got. Same thing, different day and it was frustrating because Mom, Hunter, and I had nothing to do with this. The only difference this time was that I refused to acknowledge any of them as I turned, and my eyes landed on Anais and Damien. It was almost as if a spotlight was shining on them or all of the energy in the room was coming from their direction.

It took a bit of maneuvering, but soon I found myself standing in front of the happy couple. Although I didn't know Damien terribly well due to him being older than Broderick, Gage, and Hunter, it was nice to be in the presence of a familiar face. My posture shifted, allowing me to breathe more freely, and a genuine smile appeared on my face. When

Anais looked over and saw me, she returned the expression. Damien nodded at me but said nothing.

"Hi Anais and Damien."

"Hello! Thank you so much for coming."

"Happy to. I appreciate the invite."

Anais turned and introduced me to her parents and her friend Ellie. Our conversation had devolved into small talk when I noticed Anais staring at something over my shoulder. Before I could ask what she was looking at Damien leaned over and whispered something in her ear. I turned around to see for myself but saw nothing but a sea of people.

When I turned back around, Damien and Anais were walking toward a makeshift stage. I watched as Broderick handed Damien a microphone. Instead of turning his attention to his brother, Broderick's eyes were focused on me. It was the first time I'd seen him since I'd arrived. I gave him a small smile and a wave, but all he did was nod his head in acknowledgment. *What was that all about?*

"We're going to try to get closer to the stage. Do you want to join us?"

I found Ellie on my right and shook my head. "The amount of space near the front seems somewhat small. You and her parents should go."

The excuse flew out of my mouth like a runaway train. I hadn't even given proper thought to what I was saying before I said it, but a feeling had taken over me. Something told me that Broderick was acting strange, and I didn't want to be near him right now and I was happy to oblige.

Ellie nodded before she and Anais's parents left me standing on the other side of the room just as Martin Cross got up on stage. It was clear that he would be the one to introduce his son and soon-to-be daughter-in-law to the crowd.

I watched as Martin and Damien spoke to the crowd. When the round of applause signaled that the speeches were over, I looked to see if I spotted anyone that I wanted to talk to but saw no one. While everyone's attention was still on the stage, I made my way over to the bar. When the bartender handed me the rum and Coke I ordered, something I talked myself into because I felt I needed something stronger to get through this evening, I took a sip through the dainty straw, confirming that I'd made the right choice.

I heard a throat clearing to the left of me. A quick look in that direction showed me that a tall man with dirty blond hair was standing next to me. When he sent a smirk my way, I knew what this was more than likely going to be about.

"Good evening."

"Hello," I replied, trying to appear polite, but not overly friendly. I was already on edge from attending the party; I didn't want to have to deal with whatever was on this man's agenda as well. As I thought that, the hairs on the back of my neck stood up. Chalking it up to my drink, I shifted my focus back to the stranger next to me.

"I'm Todd Ross."

I caught a glimpse of him sticking his hand out before I put my drink on the counter in front of me. "Dr. Grace McCartney." I placed my hand in his, giving him a firm handshake that lasted a beat too long because he wouldn't let go of my hand. *How quickly can I get out of this situation?*

"Doctor, eh?"

"Yes." I stopped myself from rolling my eyes. It shouldn't be a surprise, especially now, for a woman to introduce herself as a doctor. *Be polite, but don't entertain. Maybe he'll get bored and walk away.*

"Are you a friend of the family?"

"I am." I made a point of answering his questions without offering much in return, hoping he would get the hint. No dice.

He smoothed back his hair with one hand—I don't know if he thought this was a sexy motion or not—before tossing a smirk my way. When he looked as if he was going to say something, I leaned in closer because the surrounding noise had picked up slightly. He spoke louder to help me hear him better. "I was wondering if I could take you out to get to know you better. Maybe some place like Elevate?"

I swallowed hard when he finished his question, but before I could respond, I felt someone's hand land on my waist. I looked up and found Broderick standing next to me. A dark smile crossed his face, almost making me feel bad for Todd for being on the receiving end. I looked at his hand that was around me and then back up at him. Broderick's hard gaze on the man chilled me to the bone. I'd never seen him looking so lethal and it set my ire off.

4

BRODERICK

I stood near one corner of the large room and watched the crowd, avoiding anyone who wanted to strike up a conversation. I was still angry about not being able to find Malcolm, but I knew I was getting closer, and I couldn't wait for him to pay. I shifted my thoughts as I could see a woman a short distance away trying to catch my attention, but I didn't give in. Small talk or fucking that stranger wasn't on the agenda tonight, but I couldn't stop the thoughts of potential extracurricular activities with the woman who just entered my parents' home. How I wished the crass images flying through my mind were on the table.

I noticed when Grace walked into the room because all eyes turned to her, whether she wanted them to or not. The way her dress flowed over her body would be enough to make anyone stop and stare, and that was before I got a glimpse at the slit that went up to her mid-thigh. Thoughts of how her legs could end up around my waist by the end of the night left my mind just as swiftly as they entered. There was no way that I was taking it there after all these years.

That didn't mean the thoughts didn't populate in my mind, however. Images of her lying across my bed had played a starring role in many dreams, but I knew it was a line I shouldn't cross. Even as someone who listened to no one. My conscience told me that no good would come of it and I valued Hunter's and Grace's friendships too much to take things there. But that never stopped the thoughts I had about bringing her into my world.

I stood by and watched as she graduated from medical school and made a name for herself in medicine. I was without a doubt confident that she was one of the best damn doctors in the world and that was why I knew Anais was in good hands when I called her to help. And I would do it again in a heartbeat.

"Broderick."

I turned my attention to my twin, who was talking enough for the two of us. I grunted in response.

"Grace has your attention?" He raised an eyebrow and watched as she walked toward the bar.

"Hardly." I knew as soon as the lie fell from my lips that a smirk would appear on Gage's face. "Don't even start."

"I have no idea what you're talking about."

"I'm sure you don't," I said, before turning my gaze back to her. I could use another drink if I was going to have to deal with my brother's shit tonight. There was a conversation topic that I wanted to talk about, but knew we couldn't here, though I knew it would get him off my back. "When you talk about why you aren't around as much, then we can venture down the path that you want to go down."

The smirk disappeared within seconds. "Hunter couldn't make it tonight?"

I shook my head in response, noting the shift in conversation, but I added nothing to it. I was too busy wondering what Grace was up to.

"You know you could go over there and talk to her, right?"

I glanced at Gage briefly before shifting my gaze back to Grace. She was ordering a drink and I noticed something out of the corner of my eye. A man was eyeing her in much the same way I was, and I could see in his eyes he was probably having similar thoughts. But was he going to make a move?

I shifted my stance slightly as I wondered what he was going to do, and my concentration was snapped when I heard Gage snicker beside me.

"Are you going to go over there and snap his neck, Ric?"

I debated whether it would be worth the consequences if I punched him in the face for shortening my name. He knew how much I detested it, yet still did it on occasion. But I didn't because there was a more pressing matter at hand.

The man was moving closer to Grace, who had been served her drink, and I knew he was going to strike. And there was no way I was going to let that happen.

"Why don't you do something useful and hold this?" I handed my empty glass to Gage and walked away before he could respond. I slowly made my way toward them, allowing the man to get in a few words.

"I was wondering if I could take you out to get to know you better. Maybe some place like Elevate?"

That's when I decided to put an end to this. I took a step closer and placed a hand around Grace's waist, pulling her to me.

"She's not going anywhere with you, so cut the bullshit. You can leave before I escort you out. I don't think either of us would want that, right?" The smile that was displayed on my lips was anything but friendly.

The man stared at me wide-eyed as his gaze jumped from me to Grace and back again. Grace was the first to speak.

"Just who do you think you are? Don't talk about me as if I'm not standing right here and I can't speak for myself. You can go to hell." I could see the flames behind her eyes. It was taking everything in her to not lash out. I loved it.

"Look, I didn't know that you two had something going on and I—"

Grace glared at me and said, "That's because we don't. Ignore him."

The man in question looked between the two of us again before taking a small step back. "I don't know what's going on here, but I know that I don't want to be a part of it."

"Excellent choice."

"See you around, Grace."

I almost growled, but he left without another word. All of my attention was now on Grace.

"How dare you."

"How dare me? He was trying to proposition you to go to Elevate."

"And? What does it matter to you? I'm an adult and can do as I please."

"I was not going to allow you to go to Elevate with him."

Grace jerked her head back before getting right in my face. "You don't allow me to do anything. Now I'm going to leave before I cause a scene and embarrass you because I don't care what they think about me." Her brown eyes were shining brighter than I'd ever seen them before and not in a good way.

"We need to talk about this."

Grace turned on her heel and walked away without a glance back at what she'd just left behind.

5

GRACE

Anger blurred my vision as I tried to get out of the reception area as quickly as possible. I wished I had been in flats, but there was nothing I could do about it now. I'd just made it past the bathroom when I heard Broderick's voice once more.

"Grace, wait right there."

"Leave me alone. I don't know what has come over you, but it's something you need to deal with, not me."

"Listen to me."

That did it. I flipped around and sneered. "Stop being an asshole. I don't have to explain myself to you." There was no way that this could be happening. Not on this day and not from him.

"When you are standing there flirting with that fucker, the hell you do."

I paused for a heartbeat, taken aback by his words. I hadn't been flirting with Todd, in fact I had been about to send him on his way, not that anything I did with the man was any of Broderick's business. My stare turned into daggers that if they could, would've struck him instantly. "What business is it of yours who I flirt with? What has gotten into you?"

"It became my business when you—Grace. Grace!"

I'd had enough and walked away again before Broderick grabbed my hand.

"Let. Me. Go."

"Grace, we should talk about this."

I scoffed. "Absolutely not. After the way you just behaved? Leave me alone."

When I tried to remove my hand from his grasp, he tightened his hold. It wasn't painful, but it was clear he was trying to keep me close to him. I was having none of it.

"Broderick." I stared at him in the eyes unflinchingly. But it was as if I was laughing instead of glaring at the man because he didn't heed the warning laced between my words.

"Grace, you aren't allowed to go to Elevate with him. Or with anyone else for that matter."

His words came out in a harsh whisper that further lit the anger coursing through my mind. "Get real. You can't tell me where I can and cannot go."

"The hell I can't. You aren't allowed in there. Do you understand me?"

My head jolted back as if I'd been slapped. There was no way that he had said that. "You can't tell me what I can and can't do and how dare you even try? I don't know who you think died and made you the boss of me, but clearly you're delusional. This conversation is over."

I turned and walked away again, thankful that the hall where we were was mostly empty. That was due to everyone coming into the room to hear what Damien and Martin had to say. There were still a few people wandering around and I wouldn't be surprised if rumors swirled about what they'd just seen. Hopefully they didn't hear much because that would be another debacle that I didn't want to deal with.

I had debated heading toward the bathroom to escape Broderick, but now I was too far away to turn back. Instead, I knew the only way out was to leave.

I rushed over to the door and gave a hurried smile to the attendant who was standing close by. When he opened the door, I rushed out, not taking much time to look at my surroundings, focusing on finding Patrick. When I saw him sitting in the driver's seat of the car that he'd brought me here in, he gave me a small wave before he started to get out. I picked up part of my dress, making sure I didn't trip going down the stairs, when someone said my name.

"Grace."

I was expecting to see Broderick behind me, trying to force me to continue the discussion that I didn't want to have with him, but I received my second shock of the evening. I felt my eyes widen briefly before turning into slits, studying the person before me.

"Dad. Now is not a good time."

"Grace, I wanted to talk to you—"

"Dad, I meant what I said. I need to leave." I walked down the stairs as my driver stood by the car door, waiting for me. He quickly opened the door for me, but I paused when I heard my father speak.

"Can I call you? Sometime next week?"

I shrugged before I looked over my shoulder. "You can try. But that doesn't guarantee that I'll answer."

I slipped into the car without another word and was relieved to see that my father didn't attempt any further contact. Soon Patrick slid into the driver's seat and pulled away from the curb. I glanced behind me and saw my father still standing where I left him before I turned and faced forward, determined to leave the evening's events behind me. The only good thing about tonight was that I didn't have to deal with endless questions about my father.

∼

"Here we are, miss."

I looked out the window and found that he was correct. We were in front of my home. The brownstone stood tall among the other homes on the block. I'd bought the condo with a portion of an inheritance that I was gifted by my grandfather's estate, and it was one of the best things I could have bought for myself. It was the perfect size for me, and I worked with a local acquaintance to design the space in the way I liked. The whites, grays, and browns that colored the home provided a neutral vibe that I liked. Once I locked my front door, I breathed a sigh of relief. I was home.

As I walked up the stairs to my condo, I opened my clutch and briefly glanced down at my phone, wondering if anyone had contacted me. I'd turned off my phone almost as soon as we pulled off, hoping to head off anyone who might want to reach out to me. I didn't want to talk to anyone right now and was determined not to do so.

The first thing to go were the heels and with some maneuvering, I was able to get the gown off too and I changed into a college T-shirt and sweatpants that I had left on my couch. Once I was able to breathe normally again, I grabbed a glass of water from the kitchen. I walked into my living room, tossed the dress over my arm, and snatched my clutch off the coffee table and my shoes off the floor. Not knowing exactly where I wanted to go, I pivoted and wandered into my bedroom.

Instead of turning on a lamp, I turned on the overhead light, allowing that to illuminate the room. I stared at my bed, wondering if it was worth going to sleep early so that I would be well rested the next day. That thought went nowhere because there was too much adrenaline coursing through my veins after the evening I had. I couldn't help but stare at my purse in my hand, wondering if I should turn my phone back on.

Instead, I placed the clutch at the foot of my bed, put the glass of water down on my dresser and put my gown and shoes back in the closet where they belonged. Then, I reclaimed my water and walked over to one of my bedroom windows and pulled back the curtains. After confirming that the street was quiet, which made sense given the time of night, I closed the curtains.

When I turned around, I stared at the clutch once again. With a slight shake of my head, I opened the clutch and pulled my phone out, giving in to the temptation. As it powered back on, I took a sip of my water bracing myself for what I might find once my device was fully functioning. As soon as my phone gained a signal, a light ping came from it and there were two things that shocked me. One was I didn't have any calls or messages from Broderick or my father. The other thing was that I had a message from Hunter. Then again, maybe he was asking about how the party went tonight.

Hunter: *You'll never guess what happened.*

I quickly typed out a response.

Me: *Well, then tell me.*

I hoped that the news he had to share with me was good. While I waited for him to type what he wanted to say, I debated whether I should tell him about running into our father this evening, but ultimately decided not to in the event that it might ruin anything he might be sharing. Telling him about my interaction with Broderick was out of the question. Although Broderick's behavior was weird, I didn't feel the need to bring Hunter into it and cause any friction between the two of them. After all, I thought I did a good job of handling it tonight. Yet the question remained regarding what had gotten into Broderick tonight.

If I knew Broderick, I knew that he was always a man with a plan. He worked methodically and from what I had seen, did the same thing in his personal life, so for him to diverge from his normal behavior was strange. If I hadn't known any better, I would have assumed he was drunk, but he hadn't shown any of the symptoms of even being tipsy, so I threw that reason out of the window.

I glanced back at my phone and saw that Hunter was typing out his response, and I couldn't stop my foot from tapping on the floor. I walked over to my dresser and grabbed my water and took a larger gulp.

Hunter: *I made partner.*

My eyes widened as I read the text message. It took rereading it three times before I processed the news.

"Get the hell out," I mumbled to myself as I quickly called my older brother.

"Hello."

"You better not be playing with me."

"Sis, why would I do anything like that? I'm not lying. I made partner."

The squeal that left my mouth couldn't be contained. I jumped up and down and almost dropped the phone. Although I'd averted that disaster, I hadn't averted the other as water splashed down the front of my shirt. I cussed.

"Everything okay?"

"Yes, I just splashed water on myself because I got excited. Hold on." I placed the phone down on my dresser along with the glass of water and quickly changed my T-shirt. Thankfully, the water spill had been contained to just my top half, so I didn't have much to clean up. "Okay, I'm back."

"Okay, good. Everything needs to be made official and then I can announce it to the world."

"I'm so proud of you!"

The same elation that I knew he felt when I graduated from medical school shined through me as I heard Hunter chuckle on the other end of the line.

"I couldn't wait to share it with you."

I grabbed a hair tie from my dresser and put my hair up into a messy bun. "Did you call Mom?"

"I did. She cried."

That wasn't surprising. Our mother tended to get emotional about things, especially about things like this, but I knew they were happy tears.

"I'm sure I can speak for both of us and say that we are so proud of you."

"Thank you! I need to do something to celebrate, but I'll figure that out later." Hunter waited a beat before he continued. "How'd tonight go? I'm so sorry I couldn't make it."

I waved him off even though he couldn't see me. "Everything was pretty good. I saw Dad there."

"You did?" The change in his tone was clear as day and I couldn't say that I blamed him.

The man had put us through a lot of shit over the years and Hunter had more firsthand knowledge due to him being older than me. I was somewhat convinced that he hadn't told me everything he knew or saw because he was trying to protect me and when I asked, he brushed me off. But there was always that nagging feeling that something was amiss.

"Yeah, he tried to speak to me, but I didn't give him a chance to."

"Good. I'm shocked he was even invited."

Same. "Maybe he wasn't and used it to get back into the Cross Family's good graces? Bad move on his part either way. Has he tried to reach out to you?"

"Nope and that's how I prefer it."

And I couldn't say that I blamed him one bit.

6

BRODERICK

I had to hunt Malcolm down and I wasn't amused about it. It had taken some digging, but what he should have known was that when I'm determined to do something, I will go to the ends of the Earth.

"You have some fucking nerve. You couldn't come to my office and meet with me in person to discuss this piece of shit that you put together?"

The way his eyes lit up told me that I was correct in thinking that this had all been a part of his plan. He wanted to irritate me enough that I would come searching for him. *But why? How does this benefit him?*

He leaned forward and looked me straight in the eye and said, "You thought you were going to one-up me. The terms in this contract right here"—he gestured with his index finger to the papers that lay on his desk—"would give you so much power over my contacts and resources, which is how I do my business. You thought I was going to sign everything over to you for this price? You're dumber than you look."

I held back a retort to his degrading comment and leaned

back in my chair. My goal was to maintain a cold facade that would give no hints about the thoughts I was having. I chuckled. "It's interesting that you think you have a choice here."

He looked taken aback by my response and I could see him slowly starting to turn a light pink. It was clear that there weren't many people who talked to him like that. "Get the fuck out of my office."

Something clicked in my head. It was the only reason I could think of why he would have tried to blindside me with these changes. "Who else are you partnering with that wants to oppose me?"

His expression changed slightly, and he probably wasn't aware that it had. But I caught it. "What part of 'get out' didn't you understand?"

I'd let the partnering question slide for a moment. "No. Because you're going to sign this contract right here."

The sneer on his face said that he had me cornered, but the joke was on him.

"I'm not going to do shit."

I'd expected him to say something along those lines, but I paused to make him think that he'd won this battle. But I was about to win the war. I grabbed my briefcase and pulled out a stack of papers that I threw in front of him.

"You're embezzling funds from deals that you're supposed to be procuring for your clients outside of the money they're already paying you and here's the proof." I watched as he scanned the documents, so I continued, "Don't worry. You can keep those papers. I have plenty of copies."

His jaw tightened. "Are you blackmailing me?"

I crossed my arms, not bothering to hide my emotions anymore. A smile played at the corner of my lips. "Nope. Just sharing that you're not getting away with any of this even if you thought you were. Now all it takes is me getting this information into the right hands and..."

His glare filled me with glee. I watched as his eyes turned back to the papers on his desk. He snatched a pen off the surface and quickly scrawled his signature down on the sections required. When he shoved the papers toward me, I laughed before my expression turned serious.

"Now, who didn't want you to sign those papers?"

"I have no idea what you're talking about."

I stood up and leaned on his desk as if it were my own. "I'm going to give you a week to cough up the name of who you're working with. If you don't, I'll kill you. If I find out before you, I'll kill you." I paused before I continued. "It was wonderful doing business with you."

"Get out of my office."

"With pleasure."

∾

"W<small>HAT GOT INTO YOUR ASS</small>?"

"Nothing? I'm not doing anything."

"That's the point. You aren't doing anything. You're staring off into the distance like someone who lost their puppy."

I raised an eyebrow at Damien before turning my head to look back over the balcony. I was at Elevate to relax and enjoy a drink out with my brother, not get pestered by him. "The next time I have the bright idea of inviting you here with me, remind me that it's a bad idea."

Damien grunted and took a sip of his whiskey on the rocks. He did nothing but stare after he finished drinking and

I could see that he wanted me to continue. I leaned over and said, "I secured a new deal."

"That's great news. So why do you look upset about it? You should be celebrating."

"Don't feel like it."

"Am I going to have to pry it out of you?"

That made me snort. "I don't think I've ever heard you say *pry*."

"Don't change the subject."

"I secured the deal by any means necessary like how Dad taught us, and I know it's going to make me more billions in the long run. How it came about doesn't make much sense to me. Malcolm tried to screw me over before he caved once I showed him the dirt that I dug up on him."

Damien shrugged slightly. "That wouldn't be the first time that we've had to do business that way."

"I know, but this time... feels different."

Silence passed between us once again and I refused to admit that he was right. There was something else on my mind. Someone else, and I didn't want to address it with him: Grace.

I hadn't tried to reach out to her since the evening of my brother's engagement party. I thought it would be pointless. I was biding my time.

"Look, if you want to talk about Grace—"

"Why would I want to talk about her?"

"Anais—"

"Gentlemen."

I turned and found Hunter McCartney standing to my right. I watched his face to see if he might have overheard

Damien mention Grace's name, but his smile told me he hadn't.

"Welcome," Damien said as he stood up. "Can we get you anything?"

"No, that's okay. I just stopped by to see if you all were here."

My eyes narrowed at him. I couldn't imagine what he was waiting to tell me that he couldn't have reached me by other means. "Why? Did something happen?"

A grin appeared on his face. "I did it. I made partner."

I stood up and held my hand out to him. Hunter had been working diligently to get that offer and now here it was. "Congratulations, Hunt. Knew you'd do it." I grinned broadly as he shook my hand and brought it in for a pound hug.

"Thanks, man. It was a lot of hours to put in, but damn it is so worth it." His smile widened, his eyes bright, and it wasn't hard to see how proud he was of himself. And he had every right to be. "Are you going downstairs?" he asked.

I paused, debating whether it made sense for me to venture downstairs. I knew Damien wasn't, but there was nothing stopping me.

Except there was.

"Nah, man. Not tonight. You?"

Hunter looked at me before looking at Damien with a grin. "Hell yeah. I'm in celebration mode. Plus, I like this fancy key we have now. I'll catch you both later."

I could see Damien nod out of the corner of my eye as I said goodbye and we both watched Hunter leave the VIP lounge. I cut my eyes over to my brother and nearly growled. "I'm glad he didn't hear you say her name."

It was Damien's turn to raise an eyebrow at me. "Are you scared of him or something?"

"Of course not. But I also don't want him to know what happened between me and his baby sister either." I was shocked that Grace hadn't told him anything about what happened at the engagement party. Hell, I was shocked that we were able to keep our exchange quiet. Nothing had gotten back to me related to Grace.

"Good point," Damien snickered.

Seeing the look on his face, I narrowed my eyes. "What do you know?"

"I know what happened at the party." Damien grinned. "Interfering in Grace's love life means that you're asking for trouble, aren't you?"

I swore and glared at him. "How the hell do you know about that? You were up on stage with Anais."

Damien's grin widened. "Anais had a... she had to use the bathroom soon after everything wrapped up. She overheard you and Grace arguing in the hall."

"Damn it," I growled. I felt like I was in the middle of a game of telephone, trying to get actual information on what was said.

Damien soon took me out of my misery, but it all boiled down to the fact that Anais heard us talking. While I trusted them not to say anything, was there anyone else who had done the same? And if so, this could end up being a bigger headache than I bargained for.

7

GRACE

I hated that son of a bitch, with every inch of my being. Could I believe I was thinking this about Broderick now? No, but his behavior had put me on edge.

Our eyes met as soon as I entered the bar. Not even the darkness of the environment could prevent the stare down that occurred. His blue eyes clashed with mine and warning bells sounded in my mind.

It was the first time I had seen Broderick in person since we last spoke at Damien and Anais's engagement celebration. It wasn't a shock for me to be invited due to my relationship with the Cross family and I was glad to attend and celebrate the happy couple. Seeing some familiar faces was usually great, especially when you're attending an event alone. I was hoping to enjoy a night off when I didn't have anything going on, but of course Broderick Cross showed up to this party as well.

Broderick had been in my life for as long as I could remember. I was seen as just the younger sister who followed them around when we were children. That faded as we got older, and I'd seen Broderick more while I was in high school and in college.

Normally, our relationship was on good terms. It wasn't unheard of that I would watch football with him and my brother when I was free. That was all ruined the night he tried to take control over who I could and couldn't speak to. I rolled my eyes and turned away, choosing to fall deeper into the crowded bar, hoping to blend in and find my brother at the same time.

I shouldn't have been surprised. My brother was hosting the party, so the chances of Broderick attending were high. The only way it would have been higher was if Hunter had asked to host the party at Elevate. After all, the two of them had been thick as thieves for decades. Deep down I knew there was a good chance that he would show up, but I also didn't want to miss out on an evening of fun all because Broderick had decided to be a prick several weeks ago.

My work schedule sometimes meant long hours, and while my job was mostly rewarding, it had its drawbacks too. Tonight, I had an opportunity to relax and here he was attempting to insert himself into my night after I told him to get lost the last time that I saw him.

While I was at Damien and Anais's engagement party, I struck up a conversation with a man in attendance. The conversation was friendly at best and Broderick came over fuming. The whole incident was very dramatic, and I was still pissed about it. Never in the time that I'd known Broderick had he ever pulled the stunt he did that night, and I wasn't sure what made him snap and the bottom line was that I didn't need Broderick fighting battles for me. Not now, not ever.

I pulled at the dark denim jacket that I had thrown on over my low-cut black shirt and jeans with black flats. The perfect outfit for me for this spring evening. I tucked a piece of my blonde hair behind my ear and smiled at the bartender when I approached. I ordered a light beer and received it immediately, basking in the fact that I didn't have to pay due to my brother having an open bar.

"There's my favorite little sister."

I smiled at the moniker. "I'm your only little sister," I said as I turned around. There standing behind me was my older brother, IPA in hand, ready to be the life of the party.

"I'm glad you could make it."

"Same, but I wouldn't miss your promotion celebration for the world. I'm so proud of you."

I leaned in to hug him and when I looked over his shoulder, I saw the only person who was currently on my shit list.

"Hey, man, congrats again on the promotion."

Broderick came around Hunter's left side while I stood on his right. It took everything in me not to roll my eyes. I waved my brother off when one of his friends called his name and all that was left were two piercing blue eyes staring back at me.

"Grace."

I let out a deep breath. "I don't want to talk to you."

"Tough shit. I want to talk to you."

He had some damn nerve. I leaned over and whispered to him, "I'm not talking to you about anything related to my personal life because it is none of your concern. Better yet, I don't want to talk to you at all. So leave."

That didn't do anything to deter him. "Hellion, if you want to experience Elevate up close and personal, all you have to do is ask. Not entertain the idea of some asshole in a cheap three-piece suit taking you there."

My mood soured. Broderick had the audacity to say these things, but I refused to sit here and tolerate it. I took another swig of my beer before I put it back down on the bar and turned to him. "Who knew how much of an asshole you could be? Wait, don't answer that. Have a good night."

I hoped the bite in my tone told him that I wanted him to have anything but. I made my way through the crowd and found my brother.

"Listen, Hunt, something came up and I need to head out," I whispered in his ear.

"Already?" The look of disappointment made me feel like shit, but I knew if I stayed, Broderick would be watching me like a hawk all night, which was disturbing, whereas my own brother wouldn't do this. I also didn't trust myself not to snap at him again. Hunter opened his arms and I stepped into his embrace. "Do you want me to walk you to the subway?"

I shook my head. "No. Don't miss out on your own party because of me. I might decide to take a cab. I'll call you later."

"You better."

I gave him one last smile before I strolled toward the door. Just before I reached it, I looked up and found Broderick staring back at me from another corner of the room. He lifted his beer in a mock salute, and I gave him my one-finger one in return. Two could play this immaturity game.

I pulled out my phone to call a car and saw that the wait time was way longer than I wanted to deal with. I adjusted my jacket over my body, applied a coat of lip gloss, and put my phone back in my purse before I wandered down the street. I had walked a couple of buildings away from the bar before I heard a low groan coming from my left. When I looked, I found a dimly lit alleyway, but I saw nothing in the darkness.

Is someone over there? Where did that noise come from?

Although fear swam through my mind, I knew I had to do something. That was when I saw someone leaning against a brick wall and it was clear that they were hurting in some way. As I started to walk into the alley, another figure appeared from the shadows and walked up to the person and the next thing I heard was a croak. The figure backed away from the person, who slowly slid down the brick wall.

Did...did I just see someone get stabbed?

A scream bubbled below the surface, and I knew if it erupted from my mouth I would draw the attention of the person still in the alleyway. Before I could emit any sound or run away, I felt a hand slip over my lips, and another around my waist as I was dragged away from the opening of the alley. That something felt warm against my lips. Since I still had the ability to fight, there was no way I was going down without one. I fought against my attacker, and I heard a grunt before someone said, "Grace, cut it out."

Broderick?

"Let me go!" I screamed, but it was mostly muffled by what I now knew to be Broderick's hand.

He continued pulling me back until he whispered in my ear, "I'm going to remove my hand, but you have to promise not to scream."

I nodded my head quickly and he did as he said he would. As he wiped his hand, removing the remnants of my lip gloss from it, I said, "Broderick, I might be able to save his life, let me go."

"Do you want to save your own? Be quiet and follow me."

8

GRACE

"Where are you taking me?" I clutched my purse close to my stomach as if it were some sort of shield to protect me from whatever Broderick was about to throw at me.

"My apartment. For now," he said in a clipped tone. Broderick's hands tightened on the steering wheel.

"I don't want to go to your apartment. Take me home."

"Tough shit." Although his silky, smooth voice had made the comment sound less condescending, there was no way I could let this go on.

And that was the comment that had done it.

His words pissed me off. "Are you fucking kidding me? You aren't the boss of me. What the hell is going on?"

My questions flew out of my mouth a smidge lower than a roar. If words could kill, Broderick Cross's head would be slumped over, not an ounce of life to be found in his body.

"Does it look like I'm fucking kidding?"

His emphasis on the word *fucking* made me pause for a moment. I'd heard him curse at other people over the years, but never had it been directed at me, even slightly. His blue eyes stared a hole into me before turning to watch the road we were traveling down. He was going as fast as NYC traffic would allow him, just above the speed limit, and I grabbed the armrest on my door when he sped up. I was convinced it was only a matter of time before the cops pulled us over.

I didn't know what to feel. Had Broderick just saved my life or endangered it?

"Don't talk to me that way."

He glanced at me again but said nothing. I didn't know what response I hoped to get out of him, but it wasn't this. Then again, maybe this was the best thing that could have happened between us at this moment.

I looked out of the side window to see if anything was amiss. Were we being followed? But I saw nothing that would indicate we were, and when I looked back at Broderick, I could see that he was doing the same. His eyes shifted from mirror to mirror quickly, not staying on any one long enough to take his attention completely off the road in front of him.

I took a deep breath to try to calm my racing heart. Things were moving a touch too fast for me to process what was going on and I didn't like it. Even when things were moving at the speed of light in the emergency room, I relied on my training, experience, and instincts to guide me through. I was out of my depth here, in a world of unknown, trying to figure out what my next move should be.

My gut told me that I should trust Broderick. After all, we'd known each other for years and he'd never done anything to make me doubt his trust. But after his behavior during our recent encounters, was I right to trust him completely?

The shrill sound that came from my phone made me jump. It was clear that my nerves were shot. I pulled out my phone and Broderick placed a hand on my knee, stopping any movement that I was about to do. My phone rang again.

"Is that a call or text?"

"I think I should be asking the questions here."

"Don't play with me, Grace. Is that a call or text?"

I glared at him, refusing to give in. Part of me felt as if this was petty, but I didn't care. None of this was okay. I couldn't decide if calling the police to come and save me was worth it or not, but knowing what I knew about the Cross family, there was a chance that the NYPD was on their payroll.

When I didn't answer, he glanced at me and said, "In either case, I don't want you telling anyone what happened tonight. At least not yet."

That caused my eyes to widen. "Are you kidding me? Broderick, we saw someone get hurt or potentially killed and you didn't let me try to help."

"And as I mentioned, it was for your own safety. I know that you have no problem putting your life on the line for someone else, but how about we try something different tonight? The attacker could have easily turned the knife on you."

I knew he was right, but it didn't mean that I liked it. I'd gone into this profession to help as many people as possible and it pained me to not have been able to help the victim.

"It was a text message by the way. Probably Hunter."

"Don't tell him."

"He'd want to know about my well-being."

"And you're going to tell him that everything is fine."

I shifted myself in my seat to get a better look at him as he pulled up to a red light. "I don't appreciate your tone of voice so knock it off."

"I didn't realize I would have to sit here and explain to you how I just saved your life."

I threw my arms up in the air before they landed back on my lap. "That's the thing, Broderick. You aren't explaining anything."

When he didn't say anything right away, I checked the notifications on my phone.

Hunter: *I'm sorry you didn't have a good time.*

Hunter: *Maybe we can catch up for drinks when I get back?*

I quickly typed out a response. It was almost too easy to come up with the lie.

Me: *I had a great time but didn't realize how tired I was. I'm sorry. But yes, we should meet up when you return. Where are you going?*

Hunter: *DC for a week and a half for work. I leave tomorrow morning.*

Me: *Okay just send me some dates and times that work for you. Congrats again!*

Hunter: *Thanks, sis.*

"Well, Hunter will be out of town for a while. He's traveling for work for two weeks."

"Good. Hopefully that puts him out of harm's way."

"What do you mean?" I asked my question slowly, as if I was unsure of the words that were leaving my mouth. "What does he have to do with any of this?"

"Potentially nothing at all."

He was being purposely vague with his answers, but at least we were no longer cussing at each other. "Just tell me what you know."

"I don't know much, but I don't think it was an accident that we saw what we did."

"Run that by me again? How do you know that it wasn't just a random attack? Maybe a burglary gone wrong?"

"Because he waited until you were close enough to potentially see just what was going on, and he didn't run off even when he was spotted."

"But it all happened so fast."

"Not that fast. Especially for someone who is trained to kill."

I did a double take. There was no way that Broderick was being serious. "It sounds like you're spinning a dangerous, fabricated story."

"Hellion, if you only knew the half of it, you'd realize that this is anything but a fairy tale."

Before I could say anything else, I saw that our ride was coming to an end. Broderick pulled into an underground garage that I recognized as the one near his apartment, effectively shutting me up for the time being.

A nervous energy sprinted around the car as Broderick parked the SUV and unlocked the doors. I stayed seated.

"I wasn't kidding about wanting to go home."

"And I wasn't kidding when I said tough shit. Now let's go."

"No." I folded my arms across my chest, ready to sit here for the long haul.

"If you don't come on, I'm leaving you here."

"Sounds good to me."

Broderick undid his seat belt and opened his door. He turned to look at me, but I didn't move. I saw a smirk slowly start to form on his face before he could hide it. He got out of the car and slammed the door behind him. He walked around the front of the car and appeared on my side, standing in front of my door. When he opened it, I still didn't move. He rested his arms above his head, leaning on the frame of the car. I resisted the temptation to look over at him to show just how much he'd pissed me off.

"I'm going to give you one last chance to step out of the car because you aren't going to like what I'm going to do if you don't."

This time I had no problem looking him dead in his eyes, blue eyes as deep as the ocean. "No. Take me home or I'll call a car."

The smirk was back before he acted. I don't know how he was able to move so swiftly, but before I could count to three, he'd undone my seat belt.

"Get away from me, Broderick."

"No." He said it in the same tone that I had used just seconds before.

He turned my body and maneuvered us in such a way that it took him mere seconds to throw me over his shoulder into a firefighter's carry.

"Have you lost your mind?" I asked just before I took a deep breath. I started beating on any part of him that I could get my hands on. It did nothing to deter him, the pounding from my hands bouncing off his muscles as if they were made of tungsten. Too bad that wasn't real.

"This is the second most sane thing I've done today. The first was dragging you away from that crime scene," he said.

"Help! Help! Someone help me!" I hoped that someone would hear me as Broderick carried me along. The only response I got back was the sound of my voice echoing in the garage.

In between one set of my screams, Broderick said, "Don't make me gag you."

"You wouldn't dare." He walked through a door and did something before turning around to take a couple of steps back. It was then I saw that we were in front of a set of elevators. I closed my eyes as I tried to prevent the dizziness that was taking over.

"I'm starting to feel sick."

"Why do you choose to question me?" I didn't answer his question, so he continued. "If you'd just done what I said, none of this would have happened."

"The same thing could be said if you'd just taken me home."

"But we both knew that that wasn't going to happen. Only one of us accepted that answer though."

"What has gotten into you? You never used to be this much of an asshole."

Once the elevator doors closed, he set me down on my feet and I looked at him straight in the eyes. It was only then that he answered me.

"You've gotten to me."

As I waited for him to elaborate on what he had just said, he crossed his arms over his broad chest, his eyes staring straight ahead. I waited to see if he would say something else, but he didn't. The conversation was over, at least on his end.

"I'm...I'm so confused."

He glanced at me out of the corner of his eye. "We can talk more when we get upstairs."

I wondered if it was wise to take a different approach to

getting the answers that I wanted. Instead of fighting with him further, I leaned back on my heels, choosing instead to watch the numbers on the elevator as we ascended. This was an opportunity to try to put the pieces that I had together and hopefully would give me enough time to come up with a plan that might get me out of this mess.

As the elevator continued on its journey, I thought about how all of this might go down. Could I trust Broderick? Outside of his new behavior, he'd given me no reason to not trust him, but I didn't know if that was naïve on my part. I knew bits and pieces of what the Cross family was involved in and rumors of what they'd done to get what they wanted. I was worried I would meet the same fate.

9
GRACE

I stepped forward into his apartment and wasn't all that shocked by what I saw. He hadn't changed much since the last time I'd been here, maybe added a painting or two, but other than that, there wasn't anything glaringly obvious that would show that he had remodeled his home.

The walls lined with exposed brick gave the apartment in the sky a more distinct look, something I hadn't expected from him when he showed it to me the first time. The dark furniture that he had filled the space with made more sense to me, given how much he enjoyed wearing dark colors. Heck, I wondered at times if it was a common trait among the Cross men since over the years when I saw them, often, they were wearing darker colors.

I let my eyes dance over the space, wondering if there might be anything I could spot that might have changed. It gave me an opportunity to take my mind off of the situation at hand and to calm my emotions before we addressed what had happened tonight, never mind what had become of our friendship over the last few weeks. I took a brief inventory of my surroundings, making note of anything that might come in handy later.

"Drink?" His question brought my attention back to him and I saw that he was holding a beer. "Although we both would probably prefer something harder, this is a good option so we can keep a clearer mind about what we need to discuss."

I shrugged and then nodded. I wondered if his words were in reference to the screaming match that we had gotten into on the way over here but decided not to push my luck. I needed to choose my battles wisely since I was the one who needed answers that currently only he could provide. After all, right now, it was the only choice I had.

I walked over to his counter and leaned my back against it just before he handed me a beer. He had popped the top off, so I took a greedy sip of the beverage, as if I hadn't had anything to drink within the last few hours.

When I drank what I wanted, I said, "I'll take a glass of water too. Seems as if I'm a little dehydrated."

While he got the glass of water, I placed my beer down on the counter and rubbed my hands on my denim-covered thighs, hoping to get rid of any moisture that had gathered on them over the last couple of hours. The motion helped ease some of the tension that I felt, giving me a chance to think clearly about what was going on. When he turned to face me, he stared at my thighs a little longer than necessary, making me shiver slightly with intrigue. I shook the reaction off, choosing to focus on the shambles that my life was in. When he handed me the glass of water, I gave him a small smile before I took a sip. I appreciated the small reprieve from the strain in our relationship for the time being as I took a longer draw from the glass. I was also determined to not let any of the drinks I was consuming take full control over my senses. I was getting out of this apartment tonight whether Broderick liked it or not.

"Shall we have a seat?"

"Why not? The quicker we get this over with, the better."

"I agree."

That might have been the first time we agreed tonight, and I considered that a win.

With us sitting down on his couch, I crossed my legs, hoping to give the illusion of appearing confident and in control even when I felt as if my world was spinning without an axis. I thrived in life when I had a plan and right now not having one with the danger that loomed right around the corner, I wasn't doing well, hence the desire to distract myself by any means necessary to get my bearings.

Before Broderick could try to take control of the conversation, I struck first. "Why don't you think this was a random attack? Weird things happen in New York City at all hours every day. This wouldn't be the first attack where there were witnesses who just happened to come across someone getting assaulted."

Broderick waited a beat before he pulled out his cell phone. He then gave it to me. "Because of this."

My eyes widened as I read the message on the device repeatedly.

Unknown Number: *It might be worth checking in on the woman you let get away.*

"What in the entire—"

"I know. I got it after I had already started following you out of the bar."

And there was another answer to a question I had. "Wait. Not before?"

"Nope. I was determined to have whatever conversation you didn't want to have."

"How lovely of you. Can't take no for an answer." I couldn't resist the snappy comment and wished I could take it back. I was still trying to maintain the peace until I got all of the answers that I wanted.

"You're damn right. Especially when it's something I want."

My eyes narrowed at him as I took another sip from my beer. His gaze never wandered, making me wonder if the double meaning I was getting from his words was accurate. It would explain his recent behavior.

"I highly doubt that needs to be discussed right now."

"What are you afraid of, Hellion?"

"For the love of everything, stop calling me that! I'm not a hellion."

"Whatever you say." He paused before he chuckled. Then, he took a draw from his beer.

"That is not appropriate right now given if what you say is right and my life is in danger."

"You're right. Have you noticed anything strange going on recently? Within the last couple of weeks."

Now we are getting somewhere. I leaned back on the comfortable couch and thought about my life over the last few weeks. Had I seen anything that had been amiss?

"Things at work have been normal...well, as normal as things can be working in the emergency room. That's pretty much all I do outside of running errands or hanging out with friends occasionally," I paused, taking another moment to review any events that stuck out in my mind. "Well, there was this one incident that I chalked up to me being paranoid."

"What was it?"

"One evening I saw a car sitting directly across the street from my condo. The driver turned off the headlights, but never exited the vehicle. Well, at least they didn't while I was watching. I didn't think much of it because there could be a few reasons why the person didn't leave their vehicle, but it did strike me as strange. Nothing illegal about it though and they could have left the car after I stopped watching. So, I thought nothing of it until just now." I stopped my rambling just in time.

"Could be something. Could be nothing, but thanks for sharing. Did you get a good look at the vehicle or the driver?"

I shook my head. "I was far enough away from the car that it looked like your stereotypical dark colored sedan. And from the angle of my window, I couldn't see the driver well. I guess I would suck as a detective."

Broderick chuckled briefly. "Hardly. You didn't know to be suspicious of the person and you couldn't see them from where you were."

He made a good point.

"Why me?" I took another sip of my beer.

"That I don't know the answer to, although I wish I did. I do think that, for the time being, you should stay with me."

I coughed as I tried to get the liquid down my throat. "Excuse me?"

"We don't know who we're dealing with out there, Grace. But we do know that this person has connected you with me and wanted either you or me or the both of us to see what he was going to do. That should be troubling enough for you to start taking precautions."

"The only thing I want to do is go home and relax. I'll be more observant about my surroundings, and I'll carry mace on me. I don't want to stay here and that is not me trying to be offensive. I would be more comfortable in my own home."

"You also have the potential to be dead in your own home as well. Is that a risk you want to take?"

I was taken aback by his candor, but that didn't stop the words from spilling out of my mouth. "I could be dead just by walking down the street. Staying here doesn't remove that risk."

"But it lowers it. I will do everything in my power to keep you safe."

His words forced me to pause, and while I appreciated his concern, I also knew how to take care of myself.

"Broderick, you can't force me to stay here."

"I can't?"

This was not a road that I was willing to travel down. "I don't think you would appreciate holding me here against my will."

"If it meant protecting you from whatever outside force is trying to harm, I'd do it in a heartbeat."

I shook my head. Where the hell was this all coming from? He didn't have the right to storm into my life and just take over everything. But arguing with him wouldn't get me what I wanted. No, I needed to think more logically about this. To give me some time, I turned on the charm, knowing damn well that what I was about to say was going to be a lie.

"We can discuss living arrangements later. What can we do now to help us find out who coordinated the attack?"

A knock on the door brought the conversation to a halt as I jumped from the sound. Before Broderick could stand, I sent him a puzzled look. Did he have plans to have company come over this late? Instead of responding, he chose to stand up and walk over to his front door. The first thought that came to my mind was that it was the attacker. But what good would it do them to knock on the door announcing their arrival?

Broderick chose not to leave me in suspense any longer and opened the door and in walked Kingston Cross. Broderick had called in the big guns to handle this.

Kingston gave me a small wave before Broderick said, "I forwarded Kingston the text message I received just before I walked out and found you."

"Sorry it took me a little bit of time to get here. I was held up wrapping up another client's case, but I came as quickly as I could."

"It's not a problem." Broderick gestured toward the kitchen. "Can I get you anything?"

"No, I'm good. Rather just get to the facts of this case so that we can start hunting this person now."

That's what I liked about Kingston, someone I had met over the years through various functions that the Cross family had put together. He got straight to the point due to his no-nonsense personality. I knew it benefited him greatly when it came to building his security company, Cross Sentinel.

Kingston sat down in a chair opposite the couch I was seated on while Broderick joined me again. Instead of allowing the space that he had given me when we were talking before Kingston arrived, he sat down right next to me, our legs lightly touching. Although there was little chance for me to feel it, I thought I could feel the heat coming from his body and I did my best to mask my desire to touch him. How could I even think about touching him after how he treated me? I shook my head once, ridding myself of the thoughts. We had more important problems we had to face.

"So, I wasn't able to track down who the owner of the phone was or the number. If I had to guess, I would assume that the device was a burner phone."

"Shit," I said, voicing my thoughts out loud.

"Hold on, I'm not done." I turned my attention back to Kingston, wishing that he had some good news to share. "I was able to track down the location of where the person made the phone call due to cell towers."

I swallowed hard. I couldn't tell if he was pausing for dramatic effect or not, but the anticipation was driving me mad.

"Well? Continue." It was driving Broderick up a wall as well.

"It came from Queens."

I nodded. "So that means the person who stabbed someone in the alleyway couldn't have been the one to send it."

"Correct, unless he somehow scrambled the data we retrieved, making it so that we wouldn't be able to track the sender's exact location."

Broderick spoke up again. "I thought this person might be working with someone else. No hard evidence to go on, but it seemed like a very coordinated effort. Something that couldn't have been a spur-of-the-moment type of thing."

I didn't disagree with him. Some planning had to have been done in order to know where I would have been and when to strike. That, however, didn't answer another question I had. "But I don't understand how the attacker would've known the street I would be walking down and how to plan the attack in the alleyway. It wasn't as if I had written down that I would only stay at my brother's celebration for a certain length of time."

"That's a good point. The only potential explanation I have is that he or she or they had eyes on you."

Kingston's answer sent a shiver down my spine. It wasn't as if I hadn't thought of that being a possibility but having someone confirm it was another matter entirely.

"Might explain that dark colored sedan you saw outside of your house."

"I was thinking the same thing, Broderick. Only thing is I haven't seen anything else like that since it happened."

"Doesn't mean that person wasn't still out there spying on you."

Kingston cleared his throat. "I'm going to need as much information as you can provide about this."

I relayed the same story that I had told Broderick about when I had seen the car. It pained me that it wasn't much, but at least it'd be something to go on. When I was done, I looked at both men in the room. Kingston was busy jotting down notes, and I found Broderick staring at me, his gaze unsettling me even more. My thoughts temporarily jumped back to his behavior that I tabled earlier and wondered if he was thinking about it too.

Before I could give that discussion another moment of my precious time, I turned to Kingston and asked, "Did you hear anything about who the victim was? Did they survive?" I gulped down more of my beer.

Kingston didn't answer for half a second as he continued to write things down on the notepad that he brought with him. When he stopped, he looked up at me. "Yes. His name was Stewart Carnaby, and no, he didn't, unfortunately."

My hand froze with the beer near my lips. There was no way that was true. I knew that it was pointless to doubt Kingston's version of events or any intel that he had found out, but that didn't mean that I wasn't in shock. There was no way that he had said the name that I thought he had.

"You can't be serious."

I don't know if I had ever seen Kingston smile and he wasn't right now. I got up again, my thoughts returning to the night of the tragic accident.

"Grace, do you know this person?"

"Sort of. He came to my hospital after getting into a car accident. The other guy in the car I couldn't save, but we were able to save him."

"Well, I hate to be the bearer of more bad news, but he passed away at the scene according to police reports."

"You've got to be kidding me." I leaned forward and put my head in my hands, trying to wrap my thoughts around what was happening. "We knew it was a hit-and-run, but now I suspect that it wasn't merely an accident."

Kingston nodded. "If I had to guess, I would think that is correct. If I had to make another assumption, I would say that it seemed as if he wasn't supposed to make it out of that accident alive, yet he did because of you. Whoever wanted him dead has now set their sights on cleaning up the loose ends."

"Which would mean me."

10
GRACE

Hearing Kingston's thoughts on the matter did little to ease the worry I felt. After all, how could it? If he was right, it was now a matter of life or death for me. Although he had left a little while ago, his thoughts and his presence remained.

Part of me knew I should trust Kingston's judgment, after all, he was more knowledgeable about this type of thing than I was, but that didn't mean I had an easy time accepting it. If what he said was true, though, there was no way that I could burden anyone else with my problems, because there was a good chance, at least in my mind, that this person was going to come after the ones I loved.

But what did Broderick have to do with any of this? Why send him a text message instead of Hunter, who was also at the same place. What was the connection that we were missing?

"Grace."

Broderick's words brought me out of my thoughts once more. "Yes?"

"I think it's wise if you stay here."

The tone of his voice told me that he wouldn't stand for any arguing, but he didn't know that I had something else up my sleeve. "Fine. I'll stay in your guest room that I assume you have."

The corner of his lip twitched. "I was expecting more of a fight. Yes, the guest room is all set up. I'll show you the way."

I grabbed my purse and followed him down the hallway where he pointed out several of the other rooms that we passed along the way. When he stopped in front of a door, he looked back at me for a split second before opening it.

The guest room was nicely designed and didn't fit the aesthetic that he had in the living area. This was much lighter in comparison, with the focus being on creams and light grays. There was a queen-size bed with nightstands on either side and gray lamps hanging from the wall. I assumed the room had a ton of natural light during the day based on the three windows in it.

"I'll get you some of my clothes to wear tonight if you want, and we can worry about any other clothes you'll need in the future."

"Great," I said with enough conviction to convince myself.

Broderick stared at me once more and I hoped he wasn't getting suspicious due to my new tendency to agree with everything he was saying. But he said nothing and left the room, soon returning with a T-shirt and a pair of sweatpants in tow.

"Everything you need for the bathroom is already in there."

"Thanks so much. I'm probably going to go to sleep now. It's been a long night."

"Okay, I'm right down the hall if you need anything."

I nodded and watched as he closed the bedroom door behind him. Once the door clicked, I let out a long breath, allowing the nervousness to leave my body. He should have known better than to assume that I would follow his rules.

∽

I WAITED until the time on my clock shifted to 2 a.m. I glanced at the clothes that Broderick gave me that were currently lying on one of the nightstands in the guest room, folded neatly as if they had never been touched. When I got out of bed, I listened closely for any noise in the apartment.

When the only thing that greeted me was silence, I looked at my phone again.

2:01 a.m.

I called a car using an app on my phone and saw that I had several minutes before it would arrive in front of Broderick's place. I hoped he had gone to bed when I heard him walk past this door a couple of hours ago and wasn't waiting for me to make my move. I thought I had been convincing when I told him I wanted to stay here. He didn't appear to doubt my intentions so why was I overthinking this now? Plus, what was the worst that could happen if he caught me? Hold me here against my will? Well, I didn't doubt he would do it if the change in his behavior toward me was any indication.

Part of me felt like a teenager attempting to sneak out of the house for the first time, but fuck that and fuck him. I don't think I've ever cursed this much in my entire life, but Broderick was driving me to doing things I wouldn't normally do.

There wasn't any time to sit back and analyze my friendship with Broderick. I needed to get out of here and if my plan to outsmart him worked, I was going to treat myself to a strong drink. Hell, I might do it even if I don't get out of here.

I put my hand on the doorknob and slowly turned it, hoping that it didn't make a sound as I twisted and pulled the door open. When it didn't, I could have cried in relief. This had to go my way.

First, I looked down the hall to his room to see if there was a light under the door that might indicate if he was still awake. Seeing none, I assumed he had fallen asleep. I looked in the opposite direction and the only thing I could see was a slight glow from the city lights shining in the living room, giving me what looked to be enough light to get out of here without having to use my phone.

I slipped out the bedroom door and closed it quietly behind me. I tiptoed down the hall, hoping that my feet wouldn't touch a creaky wooden floorboard that might give away my location. The farther I got away from his bedroom, the more I breathed easier. My confidence grew that I could get out of here without having to deal with a confrontation with Broderick.

I didn't remember seeing any sort of alarm system when we walked into his place. The closer I got to the door I tried to recall if on one of my visits to hang out with him and Hunter I had seen anything. Nothing jogged my memory, so I just went for the door.

I paused to hear if Broderick might have awoken at any point during my trek to the exit, but I still heard nothing. I slowly unlocked the door and gently turned the doorknob. The only thing I could hear was the beating of my heart in my ears. I was so close to getting out of here and it wasn't every day that a woman plotted her escape from a seven-figure apartment in New York City.

In order to prevent the light from the hallway from shining into the living area too much, I slid between a smaller space than I would normally have between the doorjamb and the door, hoping that it wouldn't give me away.

When I was completely outside of Broderick's apartment, I sprinted down the hall, not wanting to risk anyone seeing me, even though the chances of that happening at 2 a.m. was small. I probably looked like a one-night stand whose lover refused to let her stay the night, but I didn't care. All that mattered was getting outside into the fresh air and finding the car that would take me home.

When I reached the lobby, I checked the front desk and saw that the person who had been there when we arrived was gone, probably off for the night, and someone else wouldn't take their place until the morning.

Although I assumed that there were cameras in the lobby, relief flowed through me because at least I wouldn't have to talk to anyone before my car arrived. As if I spoke it into existence, I saw a car pull up in front of Broderick's building. I quickly checked my phone and found that the color of the car matched the description listed in the app, and once I was outside, I double-checked the license plates before the driver rolled down the passenger window.

"Grace?"

"Yes. That's me."

I opened my own door and slid into the car, relishing the feel of the leather seats under my fingertips. I was on my way home at last.

11

BRODERICK

I debated calling Kingston to see if he could join me before I left, but I decided against it. He would probably think I was losing it if I told him I was going to sit outside of her home and stare up at her window for however long it took.

However long it took for me to get over my anger.

But my feelings weren't receding. In fact, they were only growing.

I had a feeling that something was up when she agreed with everything I said just before I mentioned her staying here again. She gave up too easily and I knew there was way more fight in her than that. The fire in her eyes told me so.

Yet, she bent to my will without so much as a whimper.

But her eyes told the truth, and I could see the calculation behind them as I asked her if she needed anything else. So, I waited for her to make her move.

And she did.

I turned off the lights in my bedroom and lowered the brightness of my monitor in hopes that it would make it seem as if I had gone to bed. Instead, I worked on some contracts I needed to look over and traded messages back and forth with Kingston about her security. I also briefed both of my brothers about what had happened to us tonight to alert them in case anything might be headed their way. We all had our enemies, some that we shared, some that had it out for one of us specifically. That didn't change the fact that we always needed to be on guard whenever something was happening to harm either us or the family. We had decided not to alert Dad at this time but would fill him in when the time came.

Thinking it was a good idea to sit in my vehicle outside of her apartment was a mistake. One of the few that I've ever made. All it did was make me long to go up there and yell. I wanted to let her know how it didn't make sense for her to go home, where her security was nowhere near what I could provide. I wanted to drag her back to my apartment and lock her in my bedroom and throw away the key, guaranteeing that she wouldn't escape from me again. She was selfishly putting herself at risk for no reason and that angered me.

I had heard her when she snuck out of my apartment, and I decided to give her a few minutes' head start before I followed suit. It wasn't as if I didn't know where she was going so giving her the extra time to "get away" meant nothing to me. She might think she won the battle, but she was just stalling in place like a hamster on a wheel. I had enough patience to wait this out if that's what she wanted to do.

I had the option to leave now and speed off into the night, leaving any trace of her behind me. Yet, here I was, still sitting in front of her home.

The roaring of an engine took my attention off her home

for a moment before I turned my head to stare back at her window. I watched as she placed a book on her bedside table before coming over to the window. She looked outside briefly before closing her curtains, only a dull light peeking through the cracks where the fabric didn't cover. She was going to bed, and everything was okay. Grace was fine...at least for the time being.

I shifted my position, content to sit here until I knew she was about to fall asleep. Twenty minutes later, I saw the light turn off, showing that she'd stopped reading.

I started my car and glanced at the window once more before I pulled out of the parking space.

She thought she had gotten away from me and that I wasn't going to drag her back kicking and screaming.

Too bad she's dead wrong.

12

GRACE

Things were going well. Almost too well if I had to be honest with myself. I hadn't heard from Broderick since I left his home in the middle of the night a couple of days ago, and when I should be feeling a sense of comfort, I felt a sense of unease instead. I didn't know if I expected him to come after me, but he hadn't even acknowledged my disappearance.

His silence kept me on the edge of my seat. If I knew Broderick as well as I thought I did, there was only a matter of time before he would strike and when he did it would be brutal. Although the Cross brothers tended to have unique personalities, there was one thing that they all shared: the ability to hit someone where it hurt.

That line of thinking made it hard to sleep in addition to having to deal with everything else. As I went about my business and tried to move on with my life I always wondered if Broderick or the person who killed Stewart was lurking around every corner. It also seemed as if he hadn't told Hunter anything about what had occurred because

Hunter didn't bring it up to me. If my brother knew what I had seen after I left his celebration party, he would do anything in his power to get back to New York City to be with me. So, when Broderick meant for me not to tell anyone, I saw that he mostly was keeping up his end of the bargain. Obviously, Kingston knew, which made sense, because he more than likely would be investigating the circumstances surrounding this threat to me unless I hired someone else. More than once I had thought about going to the police, but if this ran deeper than just surface-level drama, which it seemed to be, I knew getting the police involved would cause more trouble.

I opened the door to my condo and shoved myself inside, happy to be home after another long shift. I had taken precautions and watched to see if I was being followed, but I saw no one. I placed my backpack that now included mace on the countertop and walked over to get some leftovers from the refrigerator. At least I hadn't worked the night shift tonight and I had gotten home at a decent hour. I was overjoyed to be able to have the opportunity to relax for the rest of the evening and try to take my mind off the stressors that were plaguing me.

Once I sat down on my couch with my dinner in hand, I grabbed the remote and turned on my television, hoping to find something easy to watch before I took a relaxing bath and headed to bed. When I landed on a show that I could tolerate watching, I heard my phone ringing inside my bag. I stood up and walked over to my belongings and snatched my phone out of its enclosure. At least it was someone sending a text message, so I hoped I didn't have to call anyone. My goal for tonight was to enjoy my evening as much as possible and to enjoy what would be a day off tomorrow. When I saw that it was Hunter, I couldn't help but smile.

Hunter: *Hey sis. Just wanted to check in and make sure everything was OK.*

Hunter did this on occasion after our father left us when we were younger, and him being the oldest he saw most of the drama that happened between our parents. He did his best to shield me from everything, but since he was also just a kid, he couldn't stop some of the mayhem from leaking, giving me an opportunity to absorb how my environment would soon change. I thought it was cute that he still did this years later.

Me: *Everything is fine. Just sitting here watching TV before I turn in for the night.*

Hunter: *This early?*

Me: *Yeah. I just want to relax and try to get to sleep early and hope to be refreshed enough to run errands tomorrow.*

Hunter: *Well, it sounds like a plan. I'll talk to you later.*

Me: *Have a good night.*

I placed my phone face down next to me and tuned out the world as I focused on what was happening on my TV screen all the while eating dinner.

An hour later after the show finished, I stood up and turned off the TV before taking my dishes to the sink and doing some last-minute chores before I turned in for what I planned to be a relaxing evening at home.

Once I was done, I walked into my bathroom and started running my bath. As the water filled the tub, I turned my phone on silent and left it on the counter, determined to disconnect from the world if only for twenty to thirty minutes. When the water was at my desired depth, I removed my clothes and slowly slid into the tub, enjoying every second as the warm water crept up my body, providing a soothing sensation as I sunk lower into the tub. One of the reasons I bought this place was for the tub. Whoever the former owners were, they had taken particular interest in making sure that the tub in the master bathroom was huge and I thanked them for it. It made me forget some of the things that I had seen at the hospital, giving me the ability to leave work at work, which was sometimes very hard to do.

At first, I didn't move, enjoying how the water felt on my tired, achy muscles. I truly didn't know if there was anything that was better than this. Thoughts of the attack and Broderick swam from my mind, giving me the opportunity to think about nothing, which was what I preferred right now. If I could stay in this tub without turning into a pile of wrinkled mush, I would.

I chuckled at the visual and sank lower into the tub before leaning my head back against the wall and closing my eyes, embracing the feeling of the warm water surrounding me. I stayed like that for who knows how long, but once the water started to cool, I almost whined in protest. If looking at my wrinkled fingers was enough, it was clear that I needed to get out of the bath and start preparing for bed.

Once I convinced myself to get out of the tub, I dried myself off and put on a robe. I walked over to my phone and checked my notifications to reconnect with the world. I told myself that I was checking to see if I had any messages from work or if there were any updates on social media, but that was a lie. I was wondering if Broderick had contacted me.

He hadn't.

But someone else had.

Voicemail: Dad

It looked as if he'd finally gotten enough courage to contact me like he said he would at Anais and Damien's engagement party. I debated whether I wanted to listen to it but shook my head. He wasn't about to ruin my evening.

I took my phone into my bedroom and changed into a pair of yoga pants and an old T-shirt. I settled down into bed and got comfortable underneath my covers before grabbing the book I had been reading over the last couple of weeks. After some time, the words blurred and I noticed I had slid further and further down into my covers, allowing them to swallow me whole. When my eyes drifted closed, I shut my book and put it back in its rightful place before falling asleep.

~

I woke up with a start. I didn't know if I had woken up on my own or if something had done the trick, but I didn't have much interest in finding out.

The first thing I noticed was that I had fallen asleep with my lamp light on and my curtains open. As quickly as I could, I closed the curtains and that was when I heard it. A pounding on my front door.

"What the heck," I muttered as I launched my body at my phone, making sure that I had it in case I needed to call someone to help me. With my phone in hand, I hurried over to my closet and grabbed a bat that I used during a brief stint of playing softball as a kid. I wasn't expecting anyone at this time of night and if someone wanted to get up close and personal with it, they could be my guest. I stuffed my phone into a small pocket in my yoga pants, almost willing the person to knock on my door again.

But they didn't.

I walked over to my door and looked through the peephole and found nothing there. Had it been all my imagination?

With the bat firmly in hand, I opened the door and looked outside, but found no one there. What I did find however was a note taped to my door.

I snatched the piece of paper and closed the door with a decisive slam, securing every lock. I shifted the bat and opened the note. I read it over several times before it fell from my hands and floated down to the floor. The large print words that were staring back up at me would haunt me for days to come.

I'm watching you.

13

BRODERICK

Normally I liked staying up later and enjoying the stillness that the nighttime usually brought in New York City. Yes, I lived in the "City That Never Sleeps," but there was a peacefulness that settled over the city at this time of night.

Well, it would be once I was off this call. I was currently on a call with different business leaders from around the world and had picked this time because it seemed to work best, and I didn't want to take this call in my office. Now I was over it.

"Does anyone have any more questions? It's time to wrap up," I said, trying not to sound as impatient as I felt. This call had gone on for longer than necessary.

Hearing agreement, the moderator said, "Sounds like this will be it. I want to thank everyone for their time."

Before another word could be said, I hung up and began typing an email to my father and brothers, giving them a quick summary of everything that had been discussed. I'd taken one for the team by being our representative on the call since I had planned on being up anyway and knew that I would look better and be able to call in a favor from any one of them after this.

The ringing of my cellphone lifted the veil of concentration that I had fallen under. I ended the call without answering, assuming that it was a wrong number and kept typing, even though something in my gut told me to see who was calling. Chances were that there was an emergency if someone was calling at this time of night. When my phone rang again, I looked down at the screen to see who it was.

Grace. I answered the phone without another thought.

"Hi, Grace."

Instead of her responding to my greeting, I heard a slight gasp on the other end, drawing all of my attention away from the laptop in front of me.

When she still hadn't spoken, I asked, "What's wrong?" Something had to be if she was calling me this late, or even calling me at all after her "great escape" from my apartment.

"I—I need you to come over to my place." Her voice was just above a whisper, and I barely heard her.

"What's wrong?"

"I can explain when you get here. How long will it take you?" Her voice sounded a little stronger, but still not like the woman who was proudly voicing her feelings just a couple of days ago.

"I'll be there in twenty-five minutes."

∼

I ENDED up arriving with just a couple of minutes to spare. I exited my car after parking and looked around, taking inventory of the cars parked on the street. It didn't hurt to take note just in case someone whoever had caused her to call me was in the vicinity.

Grace must have been waiting for me because as soon as I stepped onto her porch, I heard all of the locks disengage and the door swung open. There stood Grace looking the most distraught that I had ever seen her. Her eyes were bloodshot red, the ponytail she'd thrown her hair into had seen better days, and her clothes were wrinkled, almost as if she'd just woken up. The wild look in her eyes told me that something had spooked her, and it was only a matter of time before she'd tell me what.

"I didn't know who to call." Her eyes bore into mine before she continued. "But please follow me."

I locked the door behind me and followed her up the stairs. Notions of what she could be waiting to tell me sped through my head as we climbed the stairs and once we were in her condo, she still didn't say anything. I was trying my best to remain patient and let her tell me on her own, a change up from the tactics that I'd recently used in her presence. But not knowing what she was going to say was tempting me to break the ice.

Me even considering letting her have some space and time to come to me was out of the norm. My time was valuable and when I wanted something, I got it quickly. Yet, here I was, taking my time with her.

When the stalemate continued, I'd had enough. "Grace, tell me why you called me."

Instead of speaking, she walked over to her coffee table, grabbed a piece of paper, and came back to me. I raised an eyebrow before looking back down at the paper.

"Someone pounded on my door and that was what I found when I answered it. Happened around midnight."

"How'd they get in? They should have had an issue getting past the front door before being able to make it into here."

"I have no idea. I didn't see anyone and I—I don't know what else to do. I didn't have anyone else to call because that would be potentially putting their life in danger and that would be the last thing I wanted."

"So you called me."

She nodded before wrapping her arms around herself in what I assumed was a way to provide comfort. "I don't want to burden my mom or Hunter and for some reason, this person has tied us together anyway..." Her voice drifted off.

I wondered where her thoughts went with it. She looked like a shell of the woman I saw at my brother's engagement party.

"You need to stay with me."

Her eyes turned back to me, and she said, "I know."

"No more fighting or arguing about this?"

She shook her head. "I'm scared to stay here by myself right now. I want Cross Sentinel to get to the bottom of this. I'm afraid that this will extend beyond me and hurt the people that I love." A tear fell down her cheek, and I brushed my hand across her face, drying it just as quickly as it fell.

"We still have some logistics to work out, but pack whatever you need and let's go."

14

GRACE

I heard the door click behind me and I felt a small piece of myself leave my body as I wondered if I had made the right choice by coming here. Here I was, back in the place where I had escaped, wondering if this could be my safe haven for the time being. When my eyes met Broderick's, something told me that I was lying to myself. I held a small breath back when I saw his mouth open, caught up in what he was going to say.

"You'll need to take time off of work."

"I was already planning on doing that. I don't think there's any way I could handle high-stress situations that go on in the emergency room with my current mental state."

"Excellent choice," he said as he walked into his kitchen. "Well, you know where everything is."

"I do." My voice quivered slightly because I knew he was alluding to my leaving his home in the middle of the night. He wouldn't make me feel guilty about a decision that I made for myself even if I ended up back where I started.

"You know, I was willing to help you because we were friends, free of charge, but now I'm not so sure about that."

I closed my eyes and licked my lips. I didn't know what road he was attempting to go down, but I wasn't about to play this game. "Broderick, how long have we known each other?"

"Long enough."

"Exactly. Why is this even coming up? I thought we were friends?" What was he getting at? Would this explain his change in behavior with me?

"Things change, Hellion."

"Would you stop calling me that?"

He took a step toward me, and I unknowingly took a step back, trying to keep the distance between the two of us.

He took another step, and I stood my ground. He wasn't going to bully me and push me into a corner.

The intensity in his eyes brought back a memory, one that I had suppressed long ago but his stare had awakened it. The moment we shared together at Hunter's first apartment. The look he'd given me back then had set my mind racing, but this was different. We were alone now, in his domain, and my curiosity forced me to stand my ground instead of blowing him off.

"Why should I stop calling you that when you enjoy it? The blush on your cheeks gives you away."

The warmth in my cheeks deepened in response and I could have cursed myself because I'd proven his point. The smirk on his face said he'd noticed it too, but I didn't care. I refused to back down.

"Broderick, if you call me that one more time, I'll—"

"You'll what, Hellion?"

"I'll tell Hunter and go to the police with this whole

thing." I'd come up with that solution on the fly and was proud of it.

"No."

I raised an eyebrow at him. "No? What do you mean, no?"

"You won't do that. But what you will do,"—he lifted my head with the tip of his finger— "is let me take care of this and of you."

He can't possibly mean what I think he does. "Broderick, what part of 'I can take care of myself' don't you understand?"

"Is that still the case?" His finger left my chin and I slightly adjusted myself, so I looked him straight in the eye. Fighting fire with fire. "Would you have called me and come here if you could have handled this all yourself?"

"I called you because you know what is going on and I consider you a friend."

The look on his face was unreadable for a second before his expression shifted, presenting the calculated businessman I'd heard about, but had never been the opposite of.

"Have we ever been friends, Grace? We are connected through your brother, but other than that..."

His remark shifted the floor beneath me and I thought he had to be lying. We've been friends for years. Where was all of this going?

"Would you get to the point?"

Broderick took a step back and paced in front of me. The vibe he was giving off wasn't one of nervousness; he was in complete control of his emotions, which made me feel off-kilter because I was barely hanging on to my own.

"I want something in return for protecting you. Hell, I

didn't even get anything for saving your life after you stormed out of Hunter's job promotion celebration."

I sighed as I thought about how much I needed this to end so that I could get some sleep after a long, stressful evening. "What do you want?"

"You're a smart woman. You'll figure it out."

The condescending tone almost made me clench my fists and to stop myself from flipping out. I knew he was doing this to get a reaction out of me and I had to remain calm. I had to play the game, much like he did in his professional life, and I assumed in his personal life.

"You aren't going to make me do a damn thing. Now, excuse me—"

"Oh, you think I'll force you to do something you don't want to do?"

His words stopped me in my tracks, but instead of waiting for me to turn around or respond, he continued.

"No. You'll be begging me to put you out of your misery, begging me to give you the release that you so desire. Begging me to take you whatever way I decide to. And that's not including any retribution that I see fit to make after you snuck out of here. Make no mistake about it because I'll be collecting it all."

With that, he walked off, not giving me room to argue with him further.

***

WHAT HAVE I DONE? I thought as I looked around the guest bedroom, noting that nothing had changed since I was last here, but I sure had. The feeling that I was trapped here was more real than it had been last time because I had no plan to leave. Escaping would toss me right back into the situation I had left or potentially throw someone that I cared about into danger.

That left the complicated feelings I had about Broderick. Right now, I couldn't have cared less if whoever did this had stabbed Broderick right in the chest. Chances were the attacker would find an empty vessel, even if they had been aiming for his heart. But I cared about the devastation that losing him would cause his family. But he had to have known the dangers of what he was throwing himself into.

Wasn't staying here putting him in danger too? I didn't want anyone to get hurt, but right now it felt as if he was the only one I could turn to, yet I didn't fully trust him. He had to know the risks of what having me stay with him would mean but didn't care.

Because the only thing he wants to do is make me beg.

15

GRACE

A slight ringing in the distance forced me to float back up to the surface. I didn't want to wake up because I could have sworn I'd only just gotten to sleep. There was no way it could be morning already.

I blindly grabbed for the offending device and instead of chucking it against the wall, I stared at the screen until my eyes could make out the letters on it.

I confirmed that I had gone to sleep just two hours ago, and that it was my mother calling me. I debated whether it was worth answering the phone or not and decided that it wouldn't hurt to do so if I could keep her somewhat in the dark about what was going on. The less she knew, the better it was for everyone.

"Hey, Mom."

"Grace, I—did I wake you? I'm so sorry. I didn't know you worked the late shift last night."

My mother was the sweetest woman I knew. Even when something wasn't her fault, she'd tried to apologize for it, and it was a habit that grew on me. It took me years to work that out of my system and still sometimes I fell victim to it.

"I didn't. I just got to bed late. How's everything going? I meant to call you a few days ago, but life got busy."

I usually called Mom to check in once or twice a week, but with everything going on, it had slipped my mind. At least we had exchanged some text messages this week.

"It's okay. I figured something came up. I wanted to find out how everything went with the engagement party. I'm sorry I wasn't able to make it and told Selena so."

I kept my thoughts about how she wouldn't have really wanted to be there anyway because of Dad's shocking appearance. After all, the last thing Dr. Jill McCartney needed to hear about was her soon-to-be ex-husband when we hadn't spoken about him in months. She'd worked so hard to get to where she was now, and I wouldn't cause any setbacks by bringing him up. I did, however, continue to fill her in on the brief details I had from that night due to my early exit. I skipped over the parts that involved Broderick stalking over to me because she didn't need to know that, nor did I want to relive it.

"It sounds like it was a lovely affair."

"It was. You'll never believe who I ran into there."

Shit. I threw my hand up to my face. The words left my mouth before I could catch them. I didn't mean to lead us down this road, but here we were.

"Who?"

I had to tell her about this now and if I wasn't awake before, I was now. "Dad."

The silence on the other end of the line told me she

hadn't been expecting that news. I could hear her sigh softly before she responded, "How did that go?"

"Not well. I blew him off and he tried to call me yesterday, but I didn't answer."

"You know I didn't want your relationship with your father to blow up like this."

Lewis McCartney had gotten what was coming to him. "Mom, I know. He did this to himself. Hunter doesn't talk to him much either as far as I know. What he did to you and to the family was unforgivable."

She paused again and then said, "I forgave him, sweetie. It wasn't worth carrying that burden around and having it tear me up inside. I told him I accepted his apology a couple of months back."

Now it was my turn to be stunned. "I didn't even know you spoke."

"We don't tell you guys everything and we needed to work this out between the two of us. Didn't want to get you all up in arms about it which I know you are in right now."

She was right. I knew that since my mother was the wronged party, that I should take her at her word and believe that things were being smoothed over, but deep down, I knew I wasn't ready to forgive.

The vows my parents took included for better and for worse, and in sickness and in health, and my father had thrown them out the door like yesterday's trash. I had to give credit where it was due and say I applauded him for reaching out to my mother to talk about what happened, but it didn't mean I was ready to move past it.

"Grace, I'm not saying that you have to talk to him, but if

you do, it might ease some of the pain you feel from his actions. That's all."

"I know. I'll think about it."

"Good."

We talked for another few minutes before I hung up the phone and lay back down on the bed. I was staring at the ceiling, wondering if it made sense to try to fall back to sleep or to drown myself in coffee in hopes that it would wake me. I quickly chose the former and turned over onto my side and closed my eyes.

It couldn't have been longer than a few minutes before I heard a knock on the door. Without waiting for an answer, Broderick walked in.

"Oh, you're still in bed."

"Yes, and I could have told you that if you'd just waited for me to respond to your knock."

"My house, my rules."

I rolled my eyes and slightly shook my head, refusing to turn my body to greet him. When I didn't say anything, he continued, further annoying me.

"We're going out tonight."

If he was looking for a reaction from me, he got one. I sat up, startled that he would suggest such a thing. "I'm not going anywhere especially if someone is trying to harm me."

If I had to be truthful with myself, I wasn't worried about anyone trying to hurt me in Broderick's presence. I just didn't want to go out with him because I didn't trust what he might do... or what I might allow him to do.

"Don't worry. I promise this is something you want to go to. Mom is hosting a family dinner and I told her I was bringing you."

"Wait. You already told her I was coming without asking me? So what was the point in coming in here at all?"

"Just giving you a heads-up."

"How courteous of you, but I'm still not going." Spending time with the Cross family had always been a lovely experience for me, but I didn't think it would be this time because I wanted to gouge Broderick's eyes out.

"Be ready by 5:30 p.m."

His command completely ignored what I had just said, further enraging me. "What part of 'I'm not going' don't you understand?"

"The same part of you that didn't understand the time I told you to be ready. I'll have something waiting for you to change into."

With that, he walked back out of the room without giving me a chance to respond and closed the door behind him. I bit back a scream that was hiding in my throat, threatening to come out. But I kept my emotions together because the worst thing I could do right now was show him how much his desire to walk all over me was getting to me. But I had something in store for him tonight and if he wanted to play hardball, then so be it.

∽

"COME IN."

Hours had passed and I glanced down at my phone before the door opened to confirm the time. It was 5:30 p.m. and I hadn't moved an inch toward getting ready to go to the Cross family dinner. I glanced up from the medical journal I was reading and found Broderick standing at the door, dressed in a burgundy sweater and navy slacks. He topped the outfit off with a pair of brown shoes. I stared for a moment too long at his body and when my eyes met his, he must have realized it too because the smirk that was already on his face only grew wider.

"How had I known that you wouldn't be ready right now?"

"Because I told you I wasn't going." My comment sounded more like a question as his comment added another piece of timber to the simmering flame that was lit within me.

"You wouldn't want to disappoint my mother, would you? After all she is expecting you."

I noted his shift in tactics and had to admit that this stung a bit. I'd been too angry earlier when he mentioned Selena and her knowing that I was coming, but now guilt crept in. Selena had done a lot to help my mother when everything went to shit, and although she'd told me many times not to feel this way, I somewhat felt indebted to her.

"I'll call her and tell I won't be there," I announced, refusing to give in because I didn't want to give Broderick any satisfaction.

"Even though I just confirmed your attendance five minutes ago?" He pulled out his phone and took a couple of steps toward me. He stretched his arm out, giving me the opportunity to read his latest text message to Selena, which included him saying that I would be there. "You have an hour to get ready. I lied about the original time because I had a feeling you weren't going to do it anyway."

"You are an asshole, you know that, right?"

"I do what it takes to get what I want."

I sat up in the bed and threw my legs over the edge. "And what exactly is it that you want?"

"You."

16

BRODERICK

It was easy to see that she was stunned, and I loved it. Throwing curveballs at her was becoming a favorite activity of mine. I knew that asking her nicely would probably get better results, but I was too far gone to do anything about it now. And everything was going just how I predicted.

The advantage of knowing someone for as long as I'd known her was that a lot of the things that she did I could easily predict without having to do much research. In some ways, her decisions reminded me of some that Hunter had made over the years, yet of course she had a mind of her own and did her own thing. The increased feistiness that she had shown had been such a turn-on and I couldn't wait to show her smart-ass mouth just what I thought of it.

I didn't want someone who would roll over easily and do exactly what I said. Yet, I didn't entirely expect her to be as combative as she was being. *For as long as you know someone, it's interesting to see that there are parts to them that they keep hidden from the public. The same goes for me.*

There was a part of me that she hadn't seen, and I couldn't wait for us to explore that side together.

I checked my watch and saw that there was still plenty of time for me to get some work done while I waited on Grace to finish getting ready. I'd left the outfit I bought for her to wear in the bathroom and a part of me couldn't wait to see if she would end up fighting me on that as well.

I stopped for a moment to see if I heard any movement coming out of the guest room and when I did, I didn't bother to hide the grin on my face. With my phone in hand, I started typing out responses to emails that I had meant to get to before Grace had called me over. As I was keeping a good pace, replying to the ones that I immediately had the answer for and asking more questions when one of my employees sent a proposal for me to review.

Time flew by and just as I pressed send on another email, a notification popped up on my phone, stopping my progress.

Unknown Number: *Everything is complete.*

I immediately knew who it was once I read the message and smiled. *Good.*

"Let's get this over with."

Grace's voice startled me, but I was able to hide it well. At least until I looked up from my phone and saw what she was wearing.

I knew what I selected would look fantastic on her because everything did. It didn't matter if it was a sweatshirt and jeans, scrubs, or a ball gown. The longer black dress might have looked simple on other people, but it didn't look that way on her. The split up the leg reminded me of the eyeful that I had gotten when she walked into my parents' home to celebrate Anais and Damien's engagement. I wondered if it would be well worth throwing everything that I had planned out the window to fuck her right now.

The dress wasn't as eye-catching as the gown that she wore to the engagement party, but she still looked just as beautiful, if not even more so.

"I also have a coat for you." I gestured to the long deep red coat I'd thrown over the couch before I walked into the guest room to "remind" her about the event we were attending tonight. It matched the red lipstick that she had worn tonight. I put my phone away, picked up the coat, and walked over to her, smiling to myself about how the black heels she'd chosen from the ones I set out for her brought her slightly closer to my height.

"This is all too much."

"What is? The coat? Spring in New York City can be hit or miss."

"The dress, the shoes, the coat. I can buy my own things and I do have my own things, Broderick."

"Call it a gift from me to you. How about that?"

She said nothing else as I helped her into her coat, giving up on arguing about this. Once she was ready to go, I quickly threw mine on as well and led her to the door. I was shocked she wasn't trying to argue about what would be the inevitable, something I was growing used to with her as we spent more time together. Then again, the last time she didn't argue, she tried to outsmart me and ran away. Although I believed that with everything going on, she was frightened even when she tried to keep her emotions together for the most part when I was around.

When we were out of the apartment and into the town

car, she finally spoke. "Are we going to the Cross estate or to your parents' place in the city?"

"Place in the city. Mom apparently wanted to stay here for a couple of weeks to do some things and Dad agreed."

"I always knew Martin Cross was a smart man."

I chuckled lightly, knowing that her comment was a dig at me versus any sarcasm toward my father. "That he is. He goes after what he wants and has no problem securing it by any means necessary."

She didn't add anything else to the conversation, instead choosing to take her phone out of the purse that she'd brought along. The silence, outside of what could be heard coming from the sound filtering in from New York City's nightlife, allowed me to focus on my own thoughts.

The drive to my parents' house wasn't long and I heard Grace sigh when the car came to a stop. When we were out of the car and on our way toward the elevator, I noticed how much space Grace preferred to have between us. The distance might hurt some people, but I knew it was a small way for her to maintain control of the predicament she was in, and I wouldn't have expected anything less.

When we were standing in front of my parent's door, I noticed the fake smile she plastered on her face, just before the door swung open. My mother greeted us both with a genuine one of her own.

"You made it!" she exclaimed as she pulled Grace into her arms first. When the two broke apart, it was then that I saw that Grace's smile became real. Then Mom threw her arms around me.

"You make it seem as if you haven't seen us in twenty years."

Mom chuckled. "I don't have my boys under one roof very often anymore so I can't help but be excited. Please come in. Anais and Damien are already here."

Once we were all settled inside of the apartment, I asked my mother, "Do you want me to contact Gage?"

"Would you? I texted him earlier, but he never responded."

Odd. I looked at Grace as she walked away with Mom before turning to my phone.

Me: *Where are you?*

I waited a beat to see if he'd respond, but when he didn't, I shoved my phone back into my pocket, and as I was about to walk away, there was a knock on the door. I looked through the peephole and found my twin standing on the other side.

Without a second thought, I swung open the door and took in his appearance. Although his clothes looked fresh, his face told a different story. The bags under his eyes and the slight weight loss told me that something was up.

"Everything okay?"

"Yeah."

He was lying and frankly I was tired of the charade he was putting on. "Gage, I know you better than anyone and can tell when you're not being truthful."

"Back off."

Alarms were blaring in my mind because he rarely got defensive when I asked him about the latest things going on in his life or what he was up to. What was he trying to hide?

"I'm not going to back off until you come clean about what you're hiding and—"

"Gage, you're here!"

Mom effectively ended the conversation due to her outburst, saving Gage from more questions from me.

While Mom hugged Gage, I looked over at Grace, who was chatting with Anais. I wondered what they were talking about and before I could make a move to walk over there and find out, Mom cleared her throat.

I turned and noticed that my mom's eyebrow was raised before she sent a small wink my way and walked with Gage farther into her place with me soon trailing behind them.

∼

DINNER WAS splendid and small talk was plentiful. My hand made its way to Grace's knee, and I lightly snorted when she swatted my hand away all the while keeping a conversation going with my parents.

I couldn't help but stare at her. I wanted her even when I knew she hated my guts and wanted to be anywhere but here. Just staring at her and watching her take in everything that my parents were saying as if it was the most important thing in the world had me mesmerized. I wondered what it would be like to have her stare at me in that way while I pushed in and out of her, bringing us both to completion. Just she and I focusing on the wants and needs of one another.

A phone rang and I turned my attention to the direction it was coming from. The whole table went silent as we waited for it to be answered. I couldn't say I was surprised to find that Gage turned the noise off and stood up.

"Going so soon?" The disappointment in Mom's voice was evident and Gage's face fell slightly.

"Yea, I'm in the middle of something and need to head

out. But dinner was delicious, and I appreciate you putting this together." He walked over to Mom and gave her a big hug. Then he waved at everyone in the room and left. It didn't go unnoticed by me that he refused to look me in the eye.

"What is going on with him?" Damien asked the room, and I was glad that finally someone had said something.

Mom answered first. "I wish I knew. Martin, do you know anything about this?"

Dad shook his head. "Not a clue, but I intend to find out." He reached out and pulled my mother closer to him, providing comfort as signs of worry appeared on her face.

"Well, does anyone want to have a cup of coffee or another piece of chocolate cake before you leave?"

Grace nodded. "That's a lovely idea."

I was happy that she'd decided to speak up and stay because I knew it meant that she was slowly getting used to the shift in our relationship and how that changed her dynamic with my family. It also surprised me because I would have thought that when we first walked in here, she would have taken the opportunity that Gage presented us with and high-tailed it out of here. Yet, now she was still here, enjoying spending additional time with us. My family could be a lot and she fit in well, just like I knew she would, given the history between us all.

She glanced at me, and I felt myself harden. How could one look shift my entire mood and make me want to say fuck it all and take her right here?

17

GRACE

Once again, silence passed between us on the way back to Broderick's place. We hadn't spoken much since we left to go to his parents' apartment, and I had somewhat done my best to avoid him even when we were sitting next to each other at dinner. That proved to be pointless because as soon as the warmth of his hand touched my knee through the split of the dress I was wearing, I was half ready for him to take me on the table in front of his family. I swatted his hand away from me just as quickly as he placed it and wished for him to put it back after I had.

Yet, there was no way I was going to beg him for anything.

I could feel his stormy gaze on me although I refused to acknowledge it, much like I had done while at dinner. He didn't let his stare leave me for too long, even when I went to the bathroom to freshen up and redo my red lips. I could feel the energy around him, and I got the sense that he didn't appreciate being ignored, but I didn't care. Giving in to him even a smidge would ruin me for who knew how long and show him that he had leverage over me, but I refused to give in. Instead, I focused on my phone even though I wasn't trying to contact anyone or surf the internet. However, it gave me the perfect excuse not to engage with him.

I felt him lean over slightly and I wondered what he might do next. I assumed that he wouldn't try to do anything with a witness close by who could see and hear almost everything. The only hindrance might be the music our driver for the night was listening to.

"Are you doing this on purpose?" he whispered into my ear.

Without looking up, I replied, "I have no idea what you're talking about."

"Oh, but I think you do, Hellion. The whole ignoring me act is cute, but not enough to stop me from taking what I want."

His words sent a shiver down my spine, not due to fear, but excitement. I hated that whatever little game he was playing with me right now was getting me riled. On the other hand, the cool act that he was performing was just that: an act. And I liked knowing that.

I turned my head slightly and said, "This isn't an act."

"Is that why I can hear your heart beating rapidly from here, Doctor?"

I rolled my eyes at his quip, but drew my focus back to my phone, deciding that it was more important than arguing with Broderick for the fiftieth time in several weeks. What I didn't like was that I couldn't say that he was wrong.

Soon we pulled up to his apartment and I quickly got out of the car, not allowing Broderick or our driver to provide any assistance. As I walked toward the front entrance, a thought clouded my mind and I wondered if the person who was watching me was doing so right now. Were they waiting for me to separate myself even a smidge from Broderick? Would this be a good opportunity to strike?

The thoughts caused me to stop walking and just as I was able to force my feet to start moving again, Broderick appeared at my side and placed his hand on the small of my back. Soon he ushered me through the front door and onto the elevator that would take us to his place.

"Don't ever stop in one place for too long, especially in open spaces. We don't know if your stalker has other means to hurt you, being by yourself might have provided an opportunity for them to attack you."

I wasn't surprised that Broderick had thought of the same thing, and I knew I was being foolish when I stopped.

"Also, if you choose to leave the apartment, you're to go with a member of your security detail."

I had agreed with him about the first part of his sentence, but the next part almost made me scream. Instead, I took a deep breath and said, "I don't need a security detail, Broderick."

"It's not about whether or not you need one. You have one." His comment seemed final.

The elevator dinged, telling us that we had reached our destination. When the doors opened, I walked ahead of Broderick, in hopes that not seeing him for several seconds would help me calm down. It didn't.

I moved out of the way when we reached his front door, giving him enough room to open it. Once we both stepped inside and he'd closed the door, I unleashed my anger. "How dare you!"

"Are you going to fight me every step of the way? I'm doing this to keep you safe."

"No, you're doing it to have control over me."

Broderick shrugged slightly. "It might be a bit of both."

"You are the biggest piece of—"

"What you should be doing is thanking me for wanting to keep you safe."

"I do, but that doesn't mean you can't ask me if I think these things are a good idea instead of going forth with it and then asking questions later. That's completely—"

He cut me off once again, but this time instead of using his words, he used his lips. It was clear that I wasn't prepared for the onslaught, but I caught on quickly.

If I were younger, I would have hated myself for giving in to his kiss so quickly, but I wasn't going to deny something that I wanted as well. No thoughts, just actions as our tongues attacked one another, trying to get the upper hand in the kiss that both of us refused to give. If the kiss was this powerful now, why'd we wait so long to give in to temptation?

I flung the coat off my body and I didn't give a second thought to my phone hitting the ground with a loud thud. Hopefully the coat cushioned its fall. I pulled him closer to me by the lapels of his jacket and he gave in before backing me into the door, allowing him to get more leverage and once again taking control. I felt his hand making its way down my torso until he reached the split in my dress. He took the back of my leg, pulling it up so that it was wrapped around his waist before he reached around and grabbed my ass.

He pulled his head slightly away from my lips and I could see some of the red lipstick had been transferred to his face. I could only imagine what I looked like, but neither of us seemed to care. "You were wearing a thong this entire time."

"No, I ran back to the guest room just now and threw it on." That earned me a slap on the ass, and I moaned.

Broderick chuckled. "Good to know."

Then he got back to business and kissed me hard again. He'd maneuvered my dress up so that it was sitting near my waist and my bare ass would touch the cold door off and on, providing another overpowering sensation that was unexpected. I closed my eyes as his fingers touched the small of my back before making their way down to my thong where he gently played with the skimpy piece of fabric. What was he going to do next?

He dragged my thong down slightly before grabbing another handful of my ass and slapping it again. This time, his groan matched mine.

His hand landed on my breast and massaged it and before I could appreciate the feeling, his hand stopped moving. My eyes slowly opened and looked into his, and I knew confusion marred my face. Why had he stopped?

He leaned forward, his forehead touching mine with his eyes closed. His labored breath told me that he enjoyed what we were doing and was now trying to calm his racing heart down, just as I was.

"You should go to bed." His voice demanded that I listen to him, yet the slight quiver of his lip told me he was barely hanging on.

Part of me wanted to ask if he meant together but I held back, immediately grasping that he meant that we should go our separate ways. I nodded, agreeing with him but the nagging feeling in the back of my mind wanted to continue what we had going on.

His hands slowly slid from my body as he opened his eyes, blue meeting brown. I wished I could tell what he was thinking at this very moment, but all I had was more questions. Where was this all leading and would I be able to survive once it crashed and burned?

I nodded slightly and he took a couple of steps back, watching me as I fixed my clothes to look more presentable. I didn't bother looking him in the eye again, for fear that it would lead me to asking more questions than I was prepared to get the answers for. Instead, I grabbed my coat and with my head held high, I walked away from him, didn't bother to look back.

My first stop was the guest bathroom, and I shook my head at what greeted me in the mirror. My makeup was everywhere, and a wild look replaced my normally calm demeanor. Without giving myself a second chance to doubt myself, I turned on the faucet, deciding that the best way to rid myself of all of this was to take a quick shower. While the water heated up, I tried to remove at least some of the makeup with the objective of getting the rest of the makeup off once I was in the shower.

Within minutes, I was in the shower, enjoying the warm water that flowed down my body helping to relieve some of the stress that I felt from the evening.

I didn't waste any time staying in the shower longer than necessary and I wrapped a towel around my body before heading for the door. When I entered the hallway, I could see that Broderick was sitting on the couch in his living room, beer in hand with the television on. Only he wasn't watching what was playing on the screen in front of him. Instead, his eyes were firmly on me. Without question. Unapologetically.

I didn't say anything else before walking into the guest room and closing the door. I couldn't diagnose how I felt about all of this, but I felt better knowing that at the very least, there was a door between us for the time being.

I couldn't get the kiss out of my mind. The way he kissed me still left my mind reeling as I tried to come to terms with it, but I couldn't. Not only had I almost come apart in his arms, but I wondered if he could have made me orgasm right there on the spot.

What I was having a hard time moving past was the vulnerability that we both displayed to one another in that moment, yet I'd never felt more distant from someone outside of my father in my entire life.

18

BRODERICK

"Look what the cat dragged in. You look like shit."

I chuckled at Gage and said, "Since we look very similar, I would assume that you're talking about yourself too?"

"I won't lie and say that I haven't seen better days."

After his exit from our parents' two days ago, I'd finally tracked down my elusive twin and convinced him to come to Elevate for a quick drink or two. I'd been a little delayed in getting there so of course he ragged on me, which was what I had expected him to do.

He immediately handed me my favorite beer, somehow knowing that I wasn't in a hard liquor mood tonight. This didn't surprise me since we often were in tune with one another and could pick up on the other's feelings whether we liked it or not.

Except this time, I didn't know what was going on with Gage and I was determined to find out why.

"So do you want to skip the bullshit and get right down to the reason you asked me to come here?"

"If that's what you want to do." I took a long drink from my beer, using that time to think of how best to proceed from here. Gage was already on edge, and I didn't want to further put him out of sorts because I was trying to gather information from him. "What's up with all of the absences and leaving suddenly when it comes to family events? Everyone is worried about you."

Gage gave a small sad smile and shook his head before he replied, "It's a long story."

"I have time." Especially if it meant sorting this out.

"There's a lot I can't discuss, but I'm working on a couple of deals that require a lot of my time."

I believed him. I could tell he was being purposefully vague, but I believed him. He knew better than to lie to me because I would be able to tell in a heartbeat. "Is it something Dad put on your plate?"

I questioned who else would give him something to do that required him to look this tired or to miss this much time with family and that was the only person I could think of. Then again, Dad said he didn't know what was going on at the family dinner and he would have no reason to lie.

"Dad's not involved, no. He recently asked me about it as well."

So, Dad had followed up. Good. "How much can you tell me?"

Gage shrugged. "I've basically told you what I can right now, but when something more concrete comes about, I'll make an announcement."

It reminded me of the deal that I'd made that almost fell right off the edge if I hadn't threatened Malcolm. I too had been purposefully vague about the terms of the agreement, but it hadn't required me working longer hours than normal in order to get it done. What the hell was Gage working on that could be this big?

"Are you in any kind of trouble? You know if you are we—"

"It's nothing like that. I'm trying to lock something down and I'm hoping that it won't be too much longer before everything is in place. Then I'll fill everyone in." He took a sip from his own drink before he continued, "Now that you've interrogated me, I want to return the favor. Why did you bring Grace as your date to the dinner?"

"She's staying with me now."

Gage did a double take. "Did you pull a Damien?"

"What? No." I paused. "Not the same circumstances, but sort of."

Gage chuckled after the words flew out of my mouth. "She has you tongue-tied already?"

"Hardly." I filled him in on what had happened since the last time we spoke about Grace.

"If she's the target, yet there is some connection to you, it would make sense to examine the people that might want to harm both of you and see if there is any overlap."

I glanced at my twin out of the side of my eye. "So basically, we would be going through a list of people that would want to harm me because who would want to harm Grace? She doesn't bother anyone."

"Well, she personally might not bother anyone, but what about her family? It's no secret that both her father and grandfather aren't exactly the most well-liked people in our world."

Why hadn't I thought of that before? Probably because I was too preoccupied with getting my tongue down Grace's throat. "Now, I remember that her father was a shitty person for what he did to her mother, but I can't remember exactly what her grandfather did. Do you?"

"Some sort of Ponzi scheme that came to light several years ago when he was on his deathbed. We both know that it isn't Grace's or Hunter's fault with what went down, but that doesn't mean people won't still have a vendetta against the family. In fact, some think Lewis might have been involved, but there wasn't any evidence pointing to that."

I agreed with him completely. I pulled out my phone and sent a quick text to Kingston about an angle we could investigate before putting my phone face down on the table beside me. I knew that he had run preliminary background checks on Grace and those closest to her, but I didn't know if he'd delved back into people who might have already passed away and who could be the link that we needed to figure out who was trying to frighten her.

"Good catch."

"I do what I can, Ric."

I glared at him for using a shortened version of my name.

"But seriously, if you need anything else, let me know."

"Duly noted since it seems that you were the twin that got all of the brains."

"Ha. I've been trying to tell you that for years. Glad you've finally come to that realization."

~

I NODDED at the security guard who was currently stationed near the front door of my suite. I'd asked Kingston to send one of his men to stand guard while I went out to Elevate with Gage and within thirty minutes, someone else was guarding Grace with their life. I'd been somewhat doubtful about leaving Grace alone at all for a multitude of reasons but catching up with Gage had proved not only to be helpful in finding out what was going on with him, but I also found out a potential lead that might help me help Grace.

I opened and closed the door behind me. Grace hadn't stepped foot into the living room since I'd been gone. That wasn't surprising since she'd done her best to avoid me since dinner with my parents a couple days ago.

My phone vibrated in my pocket as soon as I walked into the kitchen, and I wasn't surprised to find a message from Kingston.

Kingston: *Good tip. We're looking into this now.*

Me: *I'm sure the list will be a mile long.*

Kingston: *Could be. Just hope this isn't a needle in a haystack, but we want to dot all of our i's and cross all of our t's.*

Me: *Completely agree.*

I stuffed my phone back into my pocket and walked down the hall. I stopped in front of the guest room door and waited, trying to see if I could hear any noise coming from within. When I did hear some shuffling, I knocked on the door. This time I waited for her to answer because I too was feeling weird about the make out session we'd had. Normally I didn't lose control of my emotions, but I had that night. A promise that I'd made vanished into thin air and I didn't know what had come over me. Yet, I didn't have time to think about it now.

"Come in," she said, and I did.

As I entered the room, she looked up at me with her soft

brown eyes, showcasing a million emotions in just a few short seconds. Fear, confusion, and sadness were just a few that I was able to pick up on.

"I just wanted to tell you the latest on what I knew about the person who is trying to hurt you." I summarized my conversation with Gage and Kingston.

Grace nodded along but didn't give any input until she said, "Is there anything more that you need from me?"

I thought for a moment before it came to me.

"We need to get everything set up for you to be able to get into Elevate."

The confused look on her face was funny, I assumed because she suspected that I was talking about the main level. I knew when what I was talking about registered with her because her eyes flew up to mine, with heat and curiosity and a smidge of darkness behind them. I wanted to explore all three until anger burst through.

"I'm not going to Elevate with you."

"But you were willing to go with that guy that was chatting you up at Anais and Damien's engagement party?"

"We are not going down this road again. This is none of your business and I'm not interested in Elevate."

I stared into her eyes until she averted them. She couldn't hide the light that I saw when I mentioned my sex club. The smile on my face refused to be turned away and I crossed my arms. She rolled her eyes, forcing my smirk to become even more pronounced.

"You don't have to answer the question because I can see that you're lying. This is going to be fun, Hellion."

When I finished my comment, my phone buzzed again, and I retrieved it from my pocket.

Kingston: *There was a package delivered to Grace's apartment. No sender on the label, but we do have a person who attempted delivery.*

"Kingston just told me that someone tried to deliver a package to your apartment, and we were able to intercept it and the person. Do you want them to open it?"

I could still see the anger rolling off her, but my change in subject took her by surprise. "If it means getting closer to finding out who's behind all this? Of course."

I quickly texted Kingston back and waited for a response. "Get dressed just in case we need to head out."

Grace raised an eyebrow at me. "Where do you think we will be going?"

"We might have to talk with the delivery person. See if they might have any leads as to who hired them."

"That makes sense." She sat up in the bed and stretched. The loungewear she was wearing left little to the imagination and showed enough skin to make me think back to a couple nights ago. She then looked back at me. "You need to leave the room."

"Do I?" I had no problem standing where I was, enjoying the view. "I don't have to go anywhere."

"Broderick," she said, and the warning in her voice was clear. Both of us were saved by the buzzing of my phone again. "What does it say?"

I read the message before I replied. "Looks like your stalker left a piece of Stewart Carnaby for you to find should you have been at your apartment."

19

GRACE

Numb. That was what could best be described as my mood as I lay on the bed staring at the ceiling. It had been about an hour since we found out that one of Stewart's fingers had been delivered to my home.

Not only did this confirm that the reason this was happening had some connection to the two men I tried to save after the car accident a while back, but it also brought on many more questions. Did these two men have a connection to me that I didn't know about? What did Broderick have to do with all this? If this murderer had no problem stepping their game up a notch by sending me the finger of someone who was deceased, what would be the next play? Should the rest of my family be brought in and have security guard them due to whatever vendetta this person now had against me?

I massaged my temples, hoping that the motion would bring some relief to the headache that was forming or some clarity in my thinking. My brother was still out of town for work so the only immediate person who could be in danger, at least in New York City, was my father. Although we were on the outs, I wanted nothing bad to happen to him so it might make sense to have a discussion around whether a guard should be offered to him. My mother had moved out of New York City a couple years ago and was now teaching at Brentson University. It was a small town in upstate New York, and she thoroughly enjoyed living outside of the city full-time with more sporadic visits with her kids.

At first, I had only feared what might happen to me, but now with this person becoming more brash in their attempts to get my attention, I now worried for my family. What worried me even more was that we still had no idea what could bring an end to all of this. Was their true motivation just to see me dead?

This headache wasn't going away, but honestly, I hadn't expected it to. I knew it was a result of even more stress that was put on me and there was no way to ease the pressure that I was under. But I knew of something that could help with this. I thought about asking Broderick if he had any ibuprofen, but that wasn't what I wanted. I wanted something spicier that I might regret in the morning, but I cared less about that right now.

I got up off the bed, opened my door, and walked into the living area of Broderick's apartment. I didn't care that he was sitting at his kitchen counter staring at his laptop doing who knows what at this time of the evening. I did my best to avoid being in the common areas when he was around, but that didn't matter right now. I could feel his eyes on me as I walked over to one of the cabinets and grabbed a glass. I took one of his expensive bottles of tequila and poured about a shot of it into the cup in front of me. I looked at him for a moment and still found his eyes on me. I raised the glass up to him in a mock salute before putting the glass to my lips and letting the smooth liquor flow down my throat.

"You could've asked me to join you."

I snorted. "Didn't want you to."

Before I could debate about whether I wanted another shot, Broderick stood up and walked over to me, gently brushing past me as he too went to grab a glass. My eyes followed him as he grabbed a bottle of premium whiskey and poured some for himself. He then lightly clinked his glass against my cup that was sitting on the counter before downing the liquor in his glass.

With a satisfied sigh he looked at me and said, "That was fun."

"I just needed to do something that would temporarily take my mind off of everything that is happening. I know this isn't the best way to go about it, right now; I don't care."

The warming sensation that I got from the liquor felt wonderful. It gave me something else to think about that had nothing to do with whether I or someone I loved was going to be killed sometime soon.

"You know, when Kingston told us what was delivered to my apartment, you didn't seem too shocked by that."

"I know. I knew that it could be something like that just because I have built up this profile of what I think this person is. Only thing I can think is this person is not the brightest. I think it's only a matter of time before they will slip up."

"What gave you that idea? Is it because they haven't realized that I am no longer staying at my apartment?"

Broderick nodded. "That's one of the things. Also, it doesn't seem to be well thought out."

I could see where he was going with this. "Yeah, it seems

pretty drastic to go from leaving a letter saying that you're watching me to then leaving someone's finger at my door."

"I agree."

I looked over at him, shocked that we'd agreed on something for the first time in what seemed like forever. For some reason that warmed me more than the liquor I'd just consumed.

My eyes drifted down to his lips, wondering what they would feel like if they touched me again. When I looked back up into his eyes, it was as if he'd read my mind because I watched as the color in his eyes turned slightly darker and his lips landed on mine.

Thoughts about what we were doing and how we'd gotten here didn't matter. All I was concerned about was getting as close to him as possible. The kiss turned frantic and soon his hands made their way down my body. He pulled away, adding a dash of space between the two of us and said, "wrap your legs around my waist."

Without giving it a second thought, I jumped slightly, and he grasped my legs firmly placing them exactly where he wanted them. My lips attacked his once more as I felt myself being carried through his home. My focus remained on him, and it wasn't until he unwrapped my legs from his body, and I landed on something soft yet firm and slightly bouncy did I realize that I was lying on my back, my body resting on his bed.

"You don't know how long I've waited for this," he said as he climbed on top of me.

"Was it since the night that the Super Bowl championship came back to New York?"

His motions ceased and he stared down at me from his vantage point. "You remember that evening?"

"Of course, I do. You looked like you wanted to fuck me even though we were in Hunter's first apartment."

A smirk crossed his lips before he was back on me, and my entire world shifted. Need, desire, and longing took over and removed any signs of rational thought. I hadn't noticed that his hand drifted down to my wrist until he enclosed it. He brought it up to my head before he released it and brought my opposite hand up to the other side of my head.

"These stay right here. Got it?"

"And if I move them?"

"I stop what I'm doing to you. And I don't think either of us wants that."

Rather than trusting myself to say the correct words, I bit my lip and closed my eyes, hoping that would be a sign that I was ready for whatever he was about to do to my body. It was.

His hands immediately went for the straps of the flimsy tank top I was wearing and ripped them from their seams, as if they were a piece of paper that had a business transaction on it that he didn't like.

"You could have just pulled the shirt over my head."

"Takes too long," he growled as he pulled the offensive material down. I hadn't been wearing a bra so that flimsy piece of clothing was the only barrier standing between the two of us and he quickly yanked the cloth down and attacked my breasts with his talented tongue. His tantalizing mouth was driving me into a frenzy, one that I couldn't get enough of, nor did I want to. The urge to pull my hands down from their position above my head was strong, but I held firm because I didn't want him to stop. Not now. Not ever.

My nipples turned into small beads, and I could feel myself growing wetter due to his ministrations, my heart felt as if it would be flung out of my chest at any moment. When he created a path of wet kisses down my body, he made sure that my breasts didn't forget who'd just conquered them. A light slap before he massaged the area he hit made me moan in pleasure and wonder how he was going to further drive me outside my mind.

His tongue soon made its way to the waistband of the shorts I had on and lightly licked a path along the material, continuing his teasing when I wished for him to go further south. I felt my arms leave their positioning and when they did, Broderick looked at me, stern glare in place.

"What did I say?"

Instead of replying, I put my hands back down and tried to relax.

"Good girl," he said in return, and went back to his mission.

He removed all of my clothing, leaving me almost bare outside of the useless shirt that was currently riding up on my abs. I watched as he took in all of me, dissecting my every curve and my every flaw. Yet I somehow felt more vulnerable because he was completely clothed.

As if he heard my thoughts, he quickly whipped his shirt over his head, allowing me to lay eyes on his muscular frame. I studied him for several seconds before his smirk reappeared and his body was back over mine, kissing me again.

His hand made its way between us, and I felt him slowly make his way to my pussy. When he reached my core, I could have cried when he finally touched my folds and he growled at his discovery. "You were hiding your wetness from me?"

"You didn't ask."

"Good point. Can't let this go to waste." He slid one finger into me, testing if I was ready for him or not. When he added a second finger, it added a new dimension to the pleasure he was giving me before he paused.

"What—"

"I said you'd beg for me, and I meant it."

The grin on his face never left as he ran a fingertip up and down my folds before he entered me once more. I sighed at the sensation he was making me feel, but in the back of my mind, I knew that any moment he could stop, and I'd be left hanging once more. The anticipation of what he might do brought me closer to completion, but I knew I wanted his member inside me when I did.

"You're enjoying this."

"No shit."

He chuckled and stopped. This time when he pulled out of me, he got off the bed and walked over to his nightstand. Soon, he tossed a condom onto the bed and dropped his pajama pants to the ground. A sliver of my tongue ran across my lips as I stared at his hard cock. I could almost hear it begging to be inside of me. He slid two fingers into me before adding a third, stretching me and making me moan out in frustration. I could have slapped him when he laughed again.

"All of this could come to an end if you do what I tell you to do." I watched as he put the condom on himself.

I couldn't take it anymore. "Please put your—"

Broderick didn't let me finish my sentence and within a millisecond, his dick was thrust into me with one swift motion, making me cry out in pleasure.

"Fuck. It's been way too long." And it had been. It was closing in on a year since I had been with anyone.

He paused before pulling out and I bit back the urge to whine. "Doesn't matter. The only thing you're going to remember is me pounding into you like this, Hellion. Right here, right now. Turn around and get on your hands and knees."

I didn't care about the nickname anymore. I did as he said, and he did as he promised.

He fucked me so thoroughly and found a new use for the tank top: as a rein. I could feel him tightening his grip on it and pulling, causing the material to grow taunt against his stomach, while his other hand remained on my waist, helping to set our pace.

A scream fell from my lips along with what I thought sounded like his name as I gave in to my eternal urge to let everything go. My body was humming to the beat of his drum and singing his praises as I got closer to the point of no return.

"That's a sound I'll never get tired of." He growled and picked up the tempo.

The sounds that were coming out of my mouth grew louder and his grunts became more pronounced, and I shouted his name when the whirlwind flew through my body at top speed. But that didn't slow him down. In fact, he increased his speed as I rode out my orgasm.

"Fuck," he said as he followed behind me and when he leaned forward to lay on me, I didn't mind our sweaty bodies touching, his chest up against my back. In fact, I felt at peace for the first time in a while as I felt his dick pulsating inside of me, evidence of what it was like to bend to Broderick's will.

20

GRACE

I could feel his finger drifting slowly up and down my arm, leaving a tingly sensation in its wake. He didn't know I was awake, and I made no effort to clue him in, enjoying this moment together. The gentle thumping of his heart in my ear, the smooth motion of his chest moving up and down, and the stillness that surrounded us. Nothing to rush off to do, nothing to fear right this second. It was just the two of us coexisting in this space and I liked it a lot.

"Are you awake?"

"I am. How did you know?"

"Your breathing pattern changed."

I lifted my head slightly off his chest to look at him. "You're very observant."

"One of my many talents." He wiggled his eyebrows slightly and I laughed. "And now you have experienced some of my others."

He wasn't kidding about that. The things he made my body do and feel were indescribable outside of the word *sensational*. "Why didn't we do this before?"

"Because I promised I wouldn't."

It was my turn to raise an eyebrow as I shifted my body so that I was no longer lying on him. "Promised who you wouldn't?"

"Myself. Your brother. Your mother's health issues and the drama with your father stopped me in recent years." He pulled himself up into a seated position with his back against the headboard.

"Wait, why?" I could feel my anger rising as my thoughts flew to what Hunter had to do with this. My parents' issues I could understand.

"Didn't want to cause any friction with Hunter. He didn't want me sleeping with his baby sister, which I could understand. I didn't want to add more stress to your life."

I too sat up and pulled the covers on the bed closer to my chest to put some distance between Broderick and me. "What makes this different now?"

"I'm older, wiser, and I know that tomorrow isn't promised. I don't hesitate to go after what I want anymore and I want you."

His eyes were trained on mine before his hand reached out to caress my cheek. He then leaned forward and laid a soft kiss on my lips; much different than the kisses he'd massacred my lips with before. This was more timid, a different pace than the one he'd been determined to set when the shift in our relationship began.

When we pulled away, I laid a hand on his cheek, enjoying the slight stubble on his skin as it pricked my hand. This same mouth had done wonders to my body just several hours ago and I couldn't wait to see what he had in store for when we met in such an intimate way again. What I saw in his eyes before frightened and excited me and my mind nor body knew which way to turn.

"Oh, I have something for you."

I watched quietly as he reached into his nightstand. When he faced me again, he had what looked to be a black key in his hand.

"What is this?"

"It's your entrance into Elevate."

I picked up the key and examined it, mesmerized by the intricate design. "It's stunning."

"We never had an item that could be used to grant people access and now we do. Of course, it was mostly a security measure, but—"

"How were you able to clear me to enter Elevate without me signing off?"

He shrugged. "Perks of being one of the owners."

I shook my head. "Of course."

"I can't wait to take you there and to take you in there."

I swallowed hard as I envisioned what it would be like to go there. I'd never been to any part of Elevate, so the whole thing would be a new experience for me. I could feel a certain level of giddiness building at the thought of attending something that was very exclusive after having been on the outskirts of this social class for years.

"Switching topics completely, I checked my phone just before you woke up. Nothing new from Kingston."

I was relieved at the change in subject, giving me something to think about other than what I felt or was starting to feel for Broderick. "Speaking of that, what about securing my family? If this person is bold enough to dismember a body, what's the next step? Because it sounds like they are upping the ante and we mentioned trying to keep everything that is going on quiet."

"We can discuss having Kingston's men watch your family, but we'll have to explain what is going on to them. And even then, they don't necessarily have to accept the security detail."

I rolled Broderick's comment around in my head before I asked, "We couldn't just have Cross Sentinel send men to watch them from a distance?" I was hesitant to explain everything that was going on to my family because I didn't know if that would cause them more harm. Hell, there wasn't much that *I* knew about what was going on, so a lot of their potential questions would remain unanswered.

"It's something that would need to be discussed with Kingston. Why don't we get dressed and then talk to him? After all, Damien and Anais should be coming over for drinks in a couple of hours."

I could sense his amusement at the puzzled look on my face. "What do you mean they're coming by?"

"I mentioned they were coming by last night."

"Did you say it before or after sex?"

"After."

I scoffed. "Didn't I fall asleep right after?"

Broderick smirked. "You did, but I mentioned it while you were still awake."

"I have no recollection of any of that."

"If you don't want them to come by, we can reschedule it."

I couldn't stop my smile from taking over my face. He'd probably think I'd lost my mind, but he'd asked my opinion on whether I wanted something versus trying to force me to do something. It reminded me of the times before he let me see into his dark side and the desire he had to control everything. "No, it shouldn't be a problem at all."

"Well, we need to get moving then."

I smiled as he moved to get up. Things were taking a turn, making me wonder when the preverbal shoe would eventually fall.

∽

My bare feet walked across the wooden planks in Broderick's place as I walked from the bedroom to the living area. It felt wonderful to take a nice relaxing shower after all the time we'd spent over the last day or so christening several rooms in his house. I smiled when my eyes landed on Broderick, who'd gotten up before me to make sure we'd had snacks and a selection of drinks ready to go so that Damien and Anais felt welcomed. I thought him trying to remain busy was quite funny given that for as long as I'd known him since he came back from college, he was never one to not have the finest selection of alcohol in his home.

"Ready to talk to Kingston?"

"Sure."

Broderick put his phone on the countertop as I walked into the kitchen. He called his cousin and while the phone rang, Broderick grabbed a couple of glasses from the cabinet.

"I just want you to try a sip of this. This is Damien's favorite brand," he said gesturing to the bottle that he'd pulled out of his collection.

I read the label and discovered that it was whiskey. If I had to guess, I would assume the bottle was expensive.

"Kingston."

"Hey, man, I'm calling to talk to you about everything I texted you about."

"Sure. Give me a second."

While we waited for Kingston, Broderick poured the rich brown liquid into each glass before handing me mine and then he took the other for himself.

"Cheers."

"Cheers," I repeated and then took a sip of the liquor. Whiskey usually wasn't high on my list of liquors that I preferred to drink, but I had to admit that it went down smooth. "It's pretty good."

Broderick nodded, but before he could say anything, we heard some noise on the other end of the line.

"I'm back. Sorry about that." Kingston's voice flowed through the speaker once again.

For some reason, him coming back to the phone made me nervous. Was I worried about what he was going to say? Scared that I would have to tell my family about everything that was going on before I was ready? I couldn't pinpoint the cause.

"No worries. Tell us what you have and if what I said in my text messages is doable."

Although Broderick hadn't shown me the messages that he sent, I realized I wasn't worried. In what past me would call a strange turn of events, I trusted that Broderick had advocated for me and my family without me knowing the full details of the conversation and I was happy to have that aspect taken off my plate.

"I have enough men on my team to do either option depending on what my client, who in this case would be Grace, would like. Of course, if you'd prefer to let her family know the reason why they are being protected we can, but there are ways that we can avoid that if necessary."

"Do you think that this is an important step that we need to take?"

I could tell that Broderick was trying to get Kingston's opinion on the matter because he and I had already discussed that it was a good idea for my family to have some sort of security around them.

"Yes, but I wonder about telling them too much."

This time I chimed in. "I agree unless you have information that might help connect the dots about who this could be, because we're basically grasping at straws and don't know where to turn."

"I do have what might be some pertinent information for you. Broderick, do you know someone named Malcolm?"

I watched as Broderick became visibly uncomfortable. I took another sip of the whiskey that he gave me, hoping that the second or two that it took for it to reach my lips and make its way down my throat would be enough to give me something to do and diffuse the increasing tension that just entered the room.

"Yes. He tried to swindle me out of a deal, and I ended up having to force him to sign a contract. What about him?"

"He has a connection to the two men that Grace ended up trying to save during one of her last shifts."

I thought I had the glass firmly in my hand, but it turned out I was wrong. It took some quick maneuvering on my end to make sure that the glass didn't go crashing down to the ground, creating an even bigger headache for us if it had.

"Please, fill us in on what you found," Broderick said.

"As you well know, Broderick, Malcolm is a very well-connected guy, and I wouldn't be surprised if he had something to do with the two car accident victims that you treated. Dennis Lennon and Stewart Carnaby were connected to Malcolm and that was the only connection I found to you both outside of familial connection, of course. I think it further solidifies a theory that the reason why this person is coming after you, Grace, is because those men weren't supposed to survive that hit-and-run. It created a bigger headache for whoever this murderer is."

I cleared my throat, hoping to get rid of the cobwebs that seemed to have settled in my vocal cords over the last couple of minutes. "Do we have any idea who made the call to kill those men? It sounds to me as if the person who hired the murderer would be the same person that is trying to get to me."

"Not necessarily." Broderick stared at me before turning his attention back to the phone. "The murderer could be trying to get revenge because you ruined their perfect kill of some sort. They don't know what the victims might have told you before they died and that you might be seen as a loose end." Hearing Broderick say that sent an ice-cold chill down my spine.

"As far as I remember, neither one of them said anything."

This time, it was Kingston's turn to respond. "Yes, but the murderer doesn't know that." He took a deep breath before he continued, "I don't know where you guys stand on increasing security around Grace, but if this person gets even more brazen, who knows what they might do next."

I didn't know how to respond to that. Did that mean that we should hire more guards to watch over Broderick's place in order to keep me safe? I did feel safe here in general and

Broderick hadn't left my sight for longer than maybe a couple hours at a time, and whenever he did that, it wasn't as if he was leaving the apartment. He would go to another part of the house and try to get some work done where there wouldn't be any disruptions.

"How much will this all cost, including the total amount it would cost to protect my immediate family without them knowing?" I wouldn't exclude my father from this, not when it was a case of life or death. I knew that it had to be expensive but having a ballpark figure would help me calculate where I could get the funds from.

"That's not something you need to worry about," said Broderick.

"What do you mean it's not something I have to worry about?"

Kingston interrupted our conversation. "Before you guys go down this path, do you have anything else you need from me?"

Broderick shook his head. "I think we're good. Thanks for the update and we'll let you know which security measures we would like to enforce."

"Excellent." With that Kingston hung up.

Before I could argue with Broderick further, there was a knock on the door. The look on his face told me he was amused at the timing of the interruption. "Looks like Anais and Damien are here."

And just like that, our argument was tabled.

21

GRACE

"You know the only reason I stopped by here to see you that evening was because of the booze you had, right?"

"It wasn't for the advice that I was about to bestow on you that would help save your relationship with Anais?" Broderick nudged me while looking at his older brother and I bit back my laughter.

Everything said he wanted to call Damien out on his bullshit but was holding back for now. Why he was, I didn't know, but it made it more amusing for Anais and me as we looked on as the two brothers bickered back and forth.

Once again, I was seeing a different side to Broderick. One that he kept to himself or only showed when he was around people he trusted. It felt wonderful to be further into his inner circle and to explore this other side of him with me being closer to him than ever.

"It's okay to admit the truth, older brother. You wanted to come to me for help versus stopping in some random bar in the city. There's no harm in admitting it."

The ribbing continued until a faint buzzing could be heard in the room. Both Cross brothers pulled out their phones and read whatever had caused them to buzz. Broderick looked up first.

"Dad wants to talk to us quickly, so we'll take his call in my office." He reached over and squeezed my hand while Damien placed a quick peck on Anais's lips before they both walked off to handle their business.

"Want to sit on the couch over there and I'll bring our snacks?" Although I was a bit awkward about it, I'd slipped into the role of hostess almost naturally in his space.

"Sure, I'll grab our drinks."

Together we shifted the gathering over to a much more comfortable arrangement and Anais sighed happily when she sank down into the couch cushions.

"Are you still doing well? I could only imagine all of the physical and emotional trauma that you've been through and still continue to deal with after having your father shot in front of you and being kidnapped, among other things."

Anais slowly nodded her head and took a sip of the red wine that Broderick had given her when she arrived. I opted for red wine as well after the whiskey Broderick had given me, choosing to nurse it so that it all didn't go straight to my head.

"The physical scars are long gone, but the emotional ones I battle with daily. Therapy has helped tremendously." She glanced down at her glass before looking back up at me. "I told Damien we should visit. He gave me an abbreviated version of what was going on with you and I wanted to stop by in case you needed anyone to talk to."

"Yeah? That's so kind of you," I said before taking a sip of the red wine that Broderick poured. I wasn't a hardcore whiskey drinker, but I loved how smooth the liquid was. The heavier liquor was needed right now. "That came out more sarcastic than intended."

Anais raised a hand. "No harm done. I really wanted to come over and check to see how you were and tell you that if you needed someone to lean on, I'm here. I...was in a similar situation that you're in now and while I don't know exactly how you're feeling, I think you and I were both thrown into a world without any preparation for what was to come and that alone is enough to make someone feel anxious or upset, not to mention having someone trying to hurt you."

It felt nice to talk to someone who shared a similar experience. Granted, I hadn't been kidnapped from my home or anything like that, but she was right. We'd both shared some traumatic experiences and that we both were trying to come to terms with. Except, I was still living through mine, wondering when and how this person would continue making my life a living hell.

"The things we go through as a result of being with men from the Cross family isn't for the faint of heart."

"Oh, Broderick and I aren't together."

"You mean, you aren't together officially." She took another sip from her wine, and I somewhat hated how matter-of-fact her comment had sounded.

"Unofficially either." Yes, Broderick and I had taken our relationship to the next level, and we were now having sex with one another, but that didn't mean we were together. At least, that part hadn't been discussed.

Anais gave me a small grin before she said, "Whatever you say."

Later that evening, after Damien and Anais left, I lay in Broderick's bed staring up at the ceiling, watching as the ceiling fan whirled around. It was calming to look at while I was trapped in my own thoughts, giving me a reason to feel somewhat relaxed given everything going on.

Broderick and I had fallen asleep a while ago, and something had woken me, but I didn't know what. With the weight of his leg slung over mine, I was trapped partially underneath him, as if he was worried I'd run away in the night.

Although I hadn't tried that stunt again, I wouldn't have blamed him for thinking I might try it again. I closed my eyes briefly as my overthinking took over before looking back at the fan, hoping that that would clear my mind.

I thought about my conversation with Anais once the men had left the room. Could something with Broderick work after all of this is said and done? Maybe once we cleared the air on several matters and the more dangerous matter was taken care of. Having fun with sex right now was fine, but it wasn't something I wanted long term and Broderick wanted me by any means necessary and that this could work out. But was it just for now or for something long term? And was I prepared for either answer?

Before I tried to settle back down, I reached over and grabbed my phone, having silenced it when we went to bed originally.

Voicemail: Dad

I glared at my phone and tossed it so that it was at the corner of my bed. Why couldn't he take a hint?

I shifted my body, causing Broderick to move in his sleep.

I had slowly fallen back to sleep when a shrilling noise forced me from the light sleep I'd fallen into. I knew it wasn't my phone ringing. I groaned and when the noise stopped, I sighed. Silence once again.

Except it wasn't for long because Broderick said, "Hello?"

I waited a beat to see if he would say anything else and when he didn't, I tried to get comfortable again and fall asleep.

"Are you sure?" I could hear and feel Broderick shuffling beside me, and I knew I wasn't going back to sleep anytime soon.

"What's wrong?"

"Don't worry about it. Go back to sleep."

I placed my hand on his shoulder. "No. Tell me what's wrong."

Broderick stared at me once more much like he did in the kitchen before Anais and Damien arrived. It didn't take much to see that something was bothering him, and I hoped that he would trust me in the same manner that he wanted me to trust him. It was easy to see that he was weighing his options and the urge for him to tell me was astronomical.

"Someone stole one of my SUVs out of the garage tonight."

22

BRODERICK

"What's up?"

"Nothing."

I knew that she was lying. Something was bothering her, and it was clear as day. "Just say it."

"I want to talk to you."

"Those are some of the most dreaded words that anyone wants to hear especially from someone they're fucking." I didn't look up from my laptop, hoping to distract myself further. I was sitting in a chair diagonally across from her and out of the corner of my eye I could see her fidgeting.

I was waiting for a response as to how my vehicle was able to be stolen from the garage without anyone knowing anything. This building's security would have to answer for it when it was all said and done. Kingston and his team were currently trying to track it down.

"Cut the bull shit."

Grace's words dragged my eyes away from the computer to look at her. "What do you want to discuss?"

"Having your car stolen can be traumatic to some

people."

"I have plenty more." I glanced back at the screen and ran a hand through my short brown hair.

She sighed. "Not the point." Grace fought the yawn that she was trying to hold in and lost. It made sense given how early it was in the morning.

"I'm not going to burst into tears about this car, Grace. Yes, I'm annoyed, but it's not the end of the world."

"Fine, then let's talk about your desire to pay for the security that will soon be in place around my family."

I closed my laptop and tossed it on the chair next to me. "What's there to discuss?"

"I don't feel comfortable having you pay for these things. I can—"

"Not the point," I said, throwing her own words back at her. "I shouldn't have said that, and I apologize. As I've said before, you don't have to do this alone. I want to shoulder some of this burden for you. If that means fronting the cost, so be it. I won't miss the money."

"You're not going to take no for an answer."

"Glad we've reached that agreement."

She tossed her blonde hair into a ponytail, and I stood up. I walked over to the couch and sat down, pulling her closer to me and tucking her into my body. Having her next to me lessened my anger some but the emotion was still there. Instead of focusing on the car, I thought about the woman in my arms. How much she'd gone through and how she was still here, strong as ever, while all of this was going on. Maybe it was her as a person or the skills she learned and perfected as a doctor that taught her not to panic in stressful situations. Whatever it was, it continued to amaze me.

Having her by my side was the best feeling in the world and there was no way that sealing any business deals could compare. It was a feeling that my father had mentioned having from being with my mother and I was starting to understand what he meant. Work wasn't the end all, be all that I had made it out to be now that I'd gotten the woman that I always wanted. But would she stay once I told her what I'd been hiding? I debated telling her the secret right now, but our moment was interrupted when my phone rang, showing a text message had been received.

I looked at the screen and said, "You've got to be fucking kidding me."

"What?"

Instead of answering her, I showed her the message on the phone.

"Is that...is that the SUV?"

Before I could answer her, my phone rang, and I put the phone on speaker. "Hey, Kingston."

"We found the SUV."

"I know. I got a picture of it from an unknown number."

"So I guess I don't need to go into detail about what condition it is in."

This time, Grace spoke up. "Someone set the car on fire?"

I pressed a couple of buttons on the phone so that I could forward the message.

Kingston mumbled a curse under his breath. "Send me the message."

I glanced down at Grace before looking back at the phone. "Already done. It's way past time that we find Malcolm."

"I couldn't have said it better myself."

23

BRODERICK

"Dad?" I had checked my phone twice before I answered, confused as to why he was calling me. It was evening and Grace and I had spent most of the day sleeping due to the excitement from the early morning hours.

"Can't I call my son?"

I chuckled. "Of course you can. I just wasn't expecting this late. How is everything?"

"Your mother is here too."

I kept my laughter to myself this time as I imagined Mom glaring at me.

"Good. Good...Wanted to call and check up on the SUV situation."

"Cross Sentinel has retrieved their car and are in the process of examining any evidence. They were able to put the fire out without having to alert any authorities so we're flying under the radar in that regard."

"Was anyone hurt?" Mom asked.

"No, no one was around when the SUV was found,

according to Kingston. I didn't waste my time going to the scene because I knew that the only thing that it would make me do is become more pissed off."

"And I'm sure you didn't want to leave Grace especially after something like that."

"Mom, I—"

It was Mom's turn to laugh. "I'm not insinuating anything."

"Now we both know that's false."

"All I'm going to say is that it's about time. That's all."

Our conversation continued and just as we were about to wrap things up, Dad said, "By the way, I appreciate everything that you've done and continue to do for Cross Industries. Whether it's taking meetings that no one wants to do or going over paperwork that your brothers tend to pass over. It hasn't gone unnoticed, Son."

The burst of pride I felt was unexpected. "Thank you very much."

"We'll let you go since I suspect you have something or someone that you want to check up on."

"Mom has gotten to you too?" The words left my mouth before I could stop them, and both of my parents laughed.

"Of course I have. That's what happens when you're closing in on over thirty-six years of marriage. We'll talk to you soon."

I didn't even bother saying goodbye in hopes that I didn't make a fool out of myself once more. I pocketed my phone and headed into the living room where I suspected Grace would be.

There I found her, staring at the television in boredom. It was clear how much Grace loved to work. She loved helping people and when we had some downtime, she'd talk about what she saw on a day-to-day basis, giving me an insight into what it was like being an emergency room doctor.

Being forced to take this time off was making her go stir crazy and in return, starting to bother me although you wouldn't know it from looking at me.

I glanced at the television and found her channel surfing again. I crossed my arms and asked, "Are you okay?"

Grace looked over from her task. "I would be if one of the thousands of channels that you have on this television actually had something interesting on it to watch."

I glanced at my laptop before looking back at her. An idea popped into my head that suddenly seemed more interesting. "It's time to put that key to good use."

I watched as her eyes sparkled before they darkened when she realized what I was talking about. I loved it.

"I'm excited to go."

I was slightly taken aback by her answer. "Oh really?"

Grace nodded and stretched. "I've been thinking about it since you gave me the key."

"Get changed and then we'll head there."

Grace stood up but paused. "I don't have anything to wear."

"Did you ever look in the closet in the guest room?"

Her eyes turned to slits. "No. Don't tell me you—"

Grace's words were cut off because she started walking before she could finish her sentence. I gave her a couple of seconds before I followed her into the room she used to sleep in.

"Broderick—"

"I brought several things just in case but knew not to get a closet full of things because it wouldn't go over well."

My words must have been reasonable because she nodded slowly before examining several of the garments in the closet. "This one looks like the dress I wore to Anais and Damien's party."

"There's a reason for that."

She turned and smiled at me over her shoulder. "Well I need to get ready."

"Yes, you do." I gave her one last lingering glance before I left the room. I had no problem leaving her this time because I knew I was in for a surprise that I couldn't wait to unwrap.

~

I couldn't keep my hands off of her. My hand was on her knee, which was peeking through the coat she wore, hiding the fact that the dress she was wearing was short. It kept my mind focused on one thing: getting her into the club and ravishing her. It would take both of our minds off of the troubles in our lives.

Soon we were swept out of the rental car that I hired with one of Kingston's men to drive and we were inside Elevate within seconds. It helped that we went in through a private entrance, allowing us to come and leave as freely as we pleased. With our new keys in hand, we both placed them on the reader to enter. The security guard that was also managing the door, nodded in my direction just before the doors opened and we stepped down the stairs. Once our coats and her purse were secured, Grace turned to me.

"What do you have planned for tonight?"

It was the first time she'd spoken since we entered the vehicle, and I could feel the nervous energy buzzing around her. It gave me a thrill that we were about to embark on something she'd never done before.

"Nothing too crazy. Do you trust me?"

"Yes," she said without hesitation.

I stared at her for a second before putting my hand on her lower back and ushering her into a room down the hallway. I'd chosen a space that I thought she would like and opened the door, allowing her to go in first with me following behind.

I'd chosen a room that contained an enormous bed, but that wasn't the only focal point. The massage table on the far side of the room was going to be part of the main event.

"This was unexpected."

"Good. I didn't choose the doctor-patient themed room, which I thought would have an interesting way to turn the tables." When I saw her eyes light up at the mention of that room, I couldn't help, but smile. "Good to know."

A light blush appeared on her cheeks before I turned the lights down low. I hoped to cause that blush to appear in another place as well. "Take off your dress and heels."

I could see the temptation for her to argue with me was there, but her curiosity won out, because she slowly unzipped the dress and let it fall into a puddle at her feet. I was greeted by her naked back and her ass in a thong, all visuals I'd grown to crave.

"Lay down on the massage table over there."

"And if I don't want to?"

There was the feisty woman I'd grown to...grown to what? I couldn't think of the word I wanted, instead I asked, "Do you want to test me?"

She looked over her shoulder yet said nothing, so I continued.

"I control your pleasure when you're down here. Now do I have to tell you again to get on the massage table?"

She slowly turned around and took her sweet time walking over to the table. Although I acted as if I was in control, it was she who had found a way to wrestle the control I was used to having away from me whether she knew it or not. Nothing I did would stop my eyes from watching her even as I walked over to help her climb up on the table. Once she was face down on the table, I laid a sheet over her naked body, preserving some of her modesty for the time being. I rolled up my sleeves and began.

The soft music in the background guided me as I rubbed a massage oil that smelt like lavender across her body. I took my time trying to make her feel as relaxed as possible. I wasn't an expert in this field, but I could feel her melting in my hands as they made their way across her body.

I leaned down and whispered in her ear, "Is there any area in particular that you want me to work on?"

She made a noncommittal noise and groaned as I hit a spot where I could feel some tightness in her muscles. I began to work that knot out before I moved onto another part of her body.

Once I worked every muscle in her body, I slowly made my way down her back and inched the sheet down without touching it as I massaged the small of her back. The lower I went, the closer I got to the more intimate parts of her that I couldn't wait to touch. I pulled the sheet down, exposing her ass to me and I saw her body tense up slightly, I assumed in an attempt to anticipate my next move. Instead,

I moved to her thighs and massaged them. I made my way down one leg and back up the other as I stopped at her thighs, taking my time to worship them before making my move.

I inched closer and closer to her pussy, making sure not to touch it yet because teasing her made this even more enjoyable. I'd touch her when I felt she deserved it.

Although she seemed to be completely relaxed, the mood in the room shifted when I heard a light growl leave her lips. "Growing impatient, Hellion?"

"What do you think?"

I moved my finger up and down her folds lightly before I stopped. "I don't think, I know I'm the one that's driving you wild, having you wish that I was fucking you with my fingers or dick. Or do you wish I was teasing you in both your vagina and ass?"

She visibly shuttered and I smiled, filing that away for later. I let my finger play with her once more, allowing her juices that seeped out to coat my fingers before I slid my finger inside of her.

The moan that left her mouth was one of relief, finally getting what her body so desperately desired. I soon added a second and then a third finger and when I felt her getting close, I let my fingers linger for a second longer before pulling out.

Her eyes flashed red when she looked back at me over her shoulder. "Is this your way of getting me to beg again?"

I unbuttoned my shirt. "You can beg if you like but my only concern is getting these clothes off so I can fuck you on that table."

She leaned her head back and smiled before sliding her

hand between her thighs. I grinned as I flung my shirt off my body soon to be followed by my pants.

"I don't want to use a condom."

My words stopped her motions briefly. "Well it's your lucky day because neither do I and I'm on birth control. Clean bill of health as well."

"Clean here as well. Get on your hands and knees."

When she did as she was told, I climbed up on the massage table and positioned her exactly where I wanted her before sinking into her center. She arched her back and moaned as I let out a heavy sigh. I was finally home.

She was mine and I made sure that my body told her so as I drove home all of the feelings that I had for her with each thrust. I grinned when I felt her explode on my dick, but that wouldn't be the last orgasm she had tonight. Not by a long shot.

My hands tightened around her waist as I showed her just who was in control of pleasuring her body. The gasps and groans that were coming from her were like a sweet song as I kept up my pace of driving into her, each time I slam into her is one more period at the end of this sentence: Mine.

"I'm going to come again!" The words rushed out of her mouth. "Holy shit!"

"Good," I said through gritted teeth. I was close too, but I wanted to pleasure her first.

When another orgasm wrecked her body, it was enough to send me to nirvana as I let my release take over. Not caring who heard the growl that emanated from my body, I paused briefly to catch my breath. Once I had, I climbed down off the table, and she turned over just before I reached down and picked her up and took her to the large bed in the room. I then walked into the bathroom connected to the room, grabbed what I needed and walked back out. I took my time cleansing her with the washcloth before tucking her in the covers and walking back into the bathroom. After I cleaned myself off, I joined her in the bed, pulling her toward me so that her head was lying on my chest.

We laid there in each other's arms, enjoying the quietness between us. Who knew how long we laid there before Grace stretched. "I'm ready to head home if you are."

I smiled at her reference to home but didn't mention it. "Sounds good to me."

The two of us got dressed, pulling ourselves together as much as we could after having life shattering sex. I held the door open for her as she walked past me and the smile that she and I shared as we walked out of the room was soon interrupted.

"Are you fucking kidding me?"

I turned around to see who had spoken and caught what felt like a rush of weight to my gut. The only thing that stopped the momentum was my back hitting the wall. However, it took me less than a second to recover before I was able to pull my body free and I swung without looking.

"Stop!"

Grace's scream stopped me from swinging again and my attacker paused too. When I looked down, my eyes widened slightly when I noticed who it was. *Hunter.*

Because I paid attention to Grace, I was surprised when Hunter tried to attack me again, further pissing me off. I was willing to listen to Grace, but if he wanted to fight, I was more than up for the challenge.

As I ducked again, Hunter growled, prepared to attack

again. This wouldn't be the first time we've gotten into a fist fight and it more than likely wouldn't be the last. Although I preferred to use my words to get my point across, sometimes letting out my aggression was well worth it.

Hunter got one hit in and as I landed my next punch, I felt myself being pulled away from him. When I looked to see who had separated us, my eyes landed on some of Elevate's security guards. About time.

When I turned toward the entrance of the club, Grace had her hands folded across her chest and she looked anything but pleased.

24

GRACE

Livid was all I could feel as I looked at the two men in front of me. One was sporting a makeshift ice pack on his head while the other was wiping at blood coming from his lip.

"How dare you both act like this? And for what?"

Hunter snarled at Broderick. "He promised that he would never go near you and he waited until I was gone to strike. Good thing I came back early."

Broderick hadn't mentioned that. I'd deal with that in a moment. "I'm not a child, Hunter. I decide who I want to be with and who I want to spend my time with." I turned to look at Broderick. "How come you didn't mention any of this?"

The dried-up blood that Broderick was still trying to clean up gave him a more rugged look. While I'd hoped to be lying back in his arms by now, it seems as if I had to deal with these two like children.

"Barely remembered it. It was years ago."

"Bullshit. You—" I watched as Hunter rose and some of the security guards from Elevate walked toward him.

"Enough!"

My yell forced both men to look at me and halted movement from either of them.

"There's a lot that you don't know, Hunter, and I suggest that both of you pull yourselves together and get over this. You're friends first and foremost and have been for years. Don't toss it away for something silly when we are all adults here. Got it?"

When neither one of them said anything, I repeated myself. Finally getting head nods from both, I straightened my dress and announced, "I'm going to get a drink from over there and enjoy some peace and quiet while you two talk it out. Then I'd like to go home."

And with that, I spun on my heel and walked over to the bar, noting to myself that I'd been referring to Broderick's place when I talked about going home.

I walked up to the bartender, one of the few people who had been allowed to remain on the top level of the club. I ordered a shot of the whiskey that Broderick mentioned was Damien's favorite because it seemed like something that could help ease some of the anxiety I was feeling even if it would only be for a short period of time.

I smiled at the bartender for a moment before looking at the men I'd left behind. At least they weren't throwing punches again, I could give them that. But they also weren't speaking to one another which was a problem. They both could be stubborn at times, but neither one was more stubborn than me and I was determined to have them hash this out before we left the club.

With a heavy sigh, I grabbed my drink and walked back

over to the two men and sat down on a couch that was in front of their two chairs.

"Am I going to have to hold both of your hands as you discuss this? How about we start with the danger that I'm in since that should be a point we all can agree on?"

Hunter's eyes darted toward me before looking at Broderick and then back at me. "What kind of trouble?"

I gave a brief rundown about what was going on with me including confessing that I didn't tell Hunter about what had happened after his job promotion celebratory party. Even Broderick chimed in at the end to give his own take on what was happening, and I felt a sense of relief as I finally confessed to what had been going on with me for the last little while. That relief didn't last long because I could see Hunter growing angry again. Except this time, it was directed at me.

"Grace, why didn't you tell me?"

"Because I didn't want to worry you or put you in any state of mind about starting and excelling at your new job. I know how much making partner means to you and there was no way I was jeopardizing that."

"That's a shitty reason. You should have felt able to trust me with information regarding your safety no matter what circumstances I was under. You don't have to deal with this type of burden alone, especially when it would end up affecting all of us."

I was taken aback by his response, but not even the alcohol running through my body could convince me that he wasn't right. I hadn't taken into consideration how not telling my family would impact them. I'd talked over having Kingston watch them from afar and that plan was slowly going into effect. But I was a coward when it came to just telling them outright and that was a misstep on my part.

"You're right. I should have been more upfront about what was going on and what that would mean for you all and for that I apologize. It was my way of protecting the ones I love."

I noticed Broderick shift in his seat out of the corner of my eye, but he didn't say anything, and I didn't address him.

Hunter stood up and removed the ice pack from his face. He opened his arms and signaled for me to give him a hug. Had everything been forgiven that easily? I placed my glass down on the side table next to me and stood up, pulling the short dress that I'd worn to Elevate down to keep my modesty. I walked into my older brother's arms and embraced the comfort that he was showing me. It reminded me of when I was a little girl, and I would trip and fall while trying to follow behind him. He would always be there to help pick me up off the ground just as much as he was there now.

"I still don't like you with Broderick, but that's something that could be tabled for another time."

I didn't have the heart to argue with him again after sharing this moment with him. I looked over to see if Broderick might have heard and when his gaze met mine, I knew he had.

∼

THE TENSION in the car that had been present when we were on our way to Elevate was gone, replaced by an uncomfortable silence that had been in place since we'd gone our separate ways from my brother. I'd convinced Hunter that it made sense for me to stay with Broderick in the meantime because his home was more secure than Hunter's and if the attacker was tailing Hunter, I didn't want him to grow suspicious of me moving in with him. He agreed begrudgingly and didn't say anything more about that, but I hadn't given him much in the way of an opportunity to do so. Once again, I was grown and could be with and sleep with whoever I wanted whether he liked it or not.

What I didn't know was how Broderick felt about this. Several times over the course of the ride, I tried to summon up the words that would help erase the silence passing between us, but nothing came to life. It all stayed tucked away underneath a big boulder that was holding me down, one that wanted to be upfront about what I was feeling yet was too afraid to say anything about it for fear of rejection. After all, no one had stayed in a relationship with Broderick for long. What made me different?

Hunter's announcement about the deal he struck with Broderick about me raised red flags too. Outside of the misogynistic deal they'd agreed to, Hunter's warning played on repeat in my mind.

It didn't take much to tie together why Hunter would have come up with this agreement with Broderick. Broderick was known for his playboy ways, and I assumed this was Hunter's way of both protecting me and preserving his friendship with Broderick in case he and I ever looked at each other as more than just friends.

But Broderick had broken his promise. Why? And why now?

Something in the back of my mind had told me that this seemed all too good to be true, even with the ever-present danger floating in the shadows in the background. And now here I was wondering if all of this would end once the threat was removed from my life.

The quietness carried on as the town car Broderick hired for the evening pulled up to his building. Once we were in his apartment, I expected Broderick to say something to me. Yet he didn't, making me wonder what was going through his mind regarding tonight.

When I saw him in the brighter light in his apartment, he was still ruggedly handsome, but it looked as if he was more injured than I noticed. His hand had dry blood along the knuckles.

"Can you move your right hand okay?"

He flexed his hand and it seemed to be moving fine; at least there were no broken bones. I walked into the kitchen and grabbed two dish cloths and an ice pack from the freezer. Soon I was back at his side, examining his hand once more.

I gently cleaned the remaining blood from his hand before placing the ice pack on his knuckles, hoping to keep the swelling to a minimum. Broderick's other hand made its way through my hair before resting on my face and I looked into his eyes while giving a small smile. The tenderness of his uninjured hand on my cheek teased a soft smile from my lips.

"Do you have anything else you want to talk about? Let's get all of the drama out now so we can leave it behind."

Broderick thought about my question for a second before he answered. "No."

"Okay then let's head to bed. We've had enough of an adventure for one day."

25

GRACE

"Can I get you anything?" I asked on my way into the kitchen to get a drink. It was a couple of days after the incident at Elevate and I was doing my best to remain upbeat.

"No, thank you," Broderick said without lifting his head from his computer. And that's how it had been over the last couple of days.

We had no issues connecting in the bedroom after the day was done, but during the day, it seemed as if Broderick was tuning me out. I thought that things might be going on with work or that fighting with his best friend over his best friend's little sister might be a lot on anyone, but this was strange.

In all the years I've known Broderick, I've never seen him act quite like this and it was raising every red flag.

Broderick's hand was healing well, solidifying my thoughts about there not being any lasting damage. Any other marks from the fight were fading.

As I was on my way back to the guest bedroom, where I ended up working from time to time, I saw Broderick close his laptop and stand up.

"I need to head into the office for a little bit, so I'll have one of Kingston's men here to make sure nothing happens."

"Sure. Makes sense."

Maybe having him out of here for a couple hours would do me some good. Some time alone would do wonders for me. Or so I was trying to convince myself.

I heard Broderick shuffling along in his office, I assumed gathering everything he needed to head out. He stepped into the guest bedroom and gave me a quick kiss on the lips, making my doubts creep up even more. Broderick enjoyed taking his time kissing me, stirring up feelings in me with promises of what would happen sooner rather than later. But not this time.

"Security is outside, and if you need anything, I have my phone on me. I'll see you later."

He didn't wait for me to reply before he walked out, leaving me all alone in his place. *Now what should I do?*

As if it were answering my question, my phone rang dragging my thoughts with it. I reached over and grabbed my phone and found Hunter's name on my screen.

Shit, I wasn't expecting to have to deal with this right now. Shouldn't he be working? Hell, I wanted to go back to work so I could throw myself into helping people versus just sitting on my behind all day.

With a deep breath, I answered the phone. "Hey."

"I didn't know if you'd answer my call."

"You're my brother. Although I feel you were out of line,

we still have a good relationship with one another. We might have our trials, but you'll always be my brother."

"Same goes. I wanted to call and say that I apologize for what happened the other night. I got out of hand and should be held accountable for my actions. I don't necessarily like that you're with him, but if you two want to be with one another, I respect your wishes."

"I appreciate the apology, but there are some things I need to know."

Hunter paused before he said, "Feel free to ask whatever you want. It's the least I can do."

"Why are you so protective when it comes to me being with Broderick? You never really took an interest in anyone I was dating…ever."

"Are you two dating?"

His question temporarily stumped me, and he took my pause as an answer.

"That's my point, Grace. Broderick doesn't do relationships. Prefers to ride solo, and I get why he would, especially in his position."

"What position is he in?"

This time, Hunter sighed, and I could imagine that he had closed his eyes. I braced for how what he might say would impact me.

"Broderick is very much like his brothers in that if they want something, they go after it with everything they've got. I've seen him become obsessive in a way that I can't quite explain, which makes him one of the best business tycoons that New York City has ever seen. Doesn't matter what it takes, and nothing is out of the realm of possibility."

Nothing about what he said sat right with me. My thoughts drifted back to when we lay in bed, and he spoke about how he'd wanted me. If what Hunter said was true, what had he done to get me to fall into his bed?

26

BRODERICK

Lies.
Secrets.
Shadows.

Everything was getting to me, and I knew the only way out of this was to tell the truth. But would it really set me free? Maybe talking it out with Damien would be the kick in the ass I needed to fix what I had so thoroughly fucked up.

"Melissa," I said as I walked up to her desk. She'd been staring at her phone and jumped slightly before she looked up at me. "Is Damien around?"

"Um—no. You just missed him. He left about twenty minutes ago to go home."

Of course he had. Because he had someone to go home to. I debated my next move and noticed the surprised look on Melissa's face didn't shift. "Are you okay?"

She nodded curtly. "Yeah. Just saw something on my phone I didn't expect to see. Do you want me to set up some time for you to meet?"

"No. I'll call him. Thanks anyway." I left her and sent

Damien a text message on my way back to my floor. When I was seated back behind my desk, thoughts of Grace circled my mind, almost causing me to choke on any emotion I'd tried to downplay since I'd seen her the evening of Anais and Damien's engagement party.

I hid behind this computer screen because I couldn't face her. Facing her would mean facing the faults that I saw within myself and how she had inadvertently become part of this situation. No, I didn't send these assholes after her, but I had, in a way, thrown her into the lion's den.

There were some things I should have done better, but I couldn't turn back time. I'd accomplished my goal of fucking her more times than I could count and yet I still wanted more. She fit into my life perfectly, yet I knew that letting her in on something only I know right now might mean the end. And I didn't know if I could just let her go.

But it was becoming too much to bear. I wanted to give her the choice to decide, but I knew that I wouldn't like one answer over the other. How would I be able to walk out of her life if that was what she wanted me to do?

The space that I put between us did nothing to help the clarity I hoped to find. All it did was further drive me to wanting to be near her, touching and caressing her and telling her that everything was all right.

A knock on my office door forced me to shift my attention elsewhere.

"Come in."

Although I hid it, I was surprised to find Kingston standing in front of me.

Once he closed the door, I spoke. "You rarely, if ever, come to Cross Industries' offices."

"I know, but I wanted to tell you in person, because we're going to need to head over to see your pal Malcolm."

"That's why you almost look…giddy, at least it would be your definition of giddy. What did that fucker do now?"

"We just got word that he was the one that called the hit out on Grace."

I did a double take, not bothering to hide my shock. "He did what? He's usually the connector behind the scenes."

Kingston nodded. "Looks like he's had it out for you since you proposed that deal the first time. He knew about Grace's connection to you through Hunter and the icing on the cake was her trying to save the two men that he wanted dead."

My mind was spinning with this information. We were getting closer to putting an end to all of this and getting back to a sense of normalcy. Maybe this was what I could present Grace with when I came clean myself. A sense of relief came over me as I thought of the possibility. I turned to Kingston and asked, "How'd you find this out?"

"Someone dropped a tip to us, and we followed up. It's legit. He pissed off the wrong person."

"Seems to be a reoccurring behavior."

I stood up, grabbing my suit jacket before throwing it over my body. "Today is a good day for a murder. You don't fuck with what's mine."

Kingston smirked at me. "I knew you'd feel that way. I already invited him to my office to have a word about a new prospective deal that he would kill to be involved with."

∽

I wasn't shocked at how easy it was for Kingston to get Malcolm onto our turf. After all, the man was fueled by money; wherever it was, he tried to be. And now he would pay the price once he gave me the answers I wanted.

"He's come with a couple of his men, but we'll have no problem taking them out."

"Good, I would expect nothing less."

"I'm glad he's not expecting any of this."

This warehouse that Kingston kept in the middle of nowhere, outside of the hustle and bustle of the immediate city, was super handy in times like this. Too bad Malcolm should have assumed that coming out into the middle of nowhere versus meeting at one of our locations in the city was the beginning of the end. Greed had taken over his mind and it was what would eventually lead to his death.

But a sobering reminder popped into my head. How was I much different from him? I'd let my desire to consume Grace take over all rational thought and force me down a path of no return. At least that would be the case when I confessed.

The SUV that one of Kingston's men was driving pulled up to a stop in front of a warehouse that looked completely abandoned. That was a facade, however, which helped cover up the operations that were taking place behind its walls. This made it the perfect place to carry out what I wanted to do here.

The door swung open when we arrived, and I nodded at some of Cross Sentinel's finest as we walked through the dimly lit warehouse. Although it was still afternoon, the darkness of the warehouse made it feel as if it were evening. I hoped that I'd be out of here before it got anywhere close to that time because I didn't want too much traffic to slow me down from getting back to Grace.

When we reached where Malcolm was located, I spotted him before he saw me. I chuckled to myself about his confidence and how he should have known that he was walking into a trap. Even with the two men he'd brought with him, he should have known that there was no way he was making it out of here alive, but he doubted just how efficient Cross Sentinel was. What a foolish person to think that Kingston might want to have anything to do with him after he tried to screw me over. The cockiness and greed that he exhibited would be what finished him off in the end.

"Well, well, well. Fancy seeing you here," I said, announcing my arrival as I got within eyeshot of Malcolm and his guards.

"Of course it's you. What do you want?"

"Did you actually think you came here to do business with another member of my family after you tried to screw me over and then send someone after Grace?"

His eyes darted to one of his guards before looking back at me. "I have no idea what you're talking about."

"Oh really? Is this how you want to go about it?"

"Broderick, none of this has to end this way."

I scoffed. "You lost any chance of this ending in any other way outside of you leaving here in a body bag." I saw Malcolm's guards reach for their weapons out of the corner of my eye, but Malcolm held his right hand up and they settled down. He truly thought that he was still in control on my turf, and it was comical at best, stupid at worst. But I'd let it continue until I got the answers I wanted. "Now tell me why you sent someone after Grace?"

"Dennis Lennon and Stewart Carnaby stole from me and were supposed to pay the price for it. I knew that she was one of the doctors that saved Stewart's life and I wasn't sure if he'd told her anything because he's been known to leave little clues in places as an insurance policy. It didn't take much to connect her to you because everyone knows your connection to Hunter."

"So that's why you needed to get rid of her."

Malcolm shrugged. "It didn't help that she might also tell you some of the information that Stewart might have known. Would have given you more leverage over me."

The urge to hit him was strong, but I was determined to keep my cool. Couldn't show all my cards before I was ready. "So you sent the text message to me so that we'd both see your hitman kill Stewart."

His smile would have probably made most people shrink back in fright, but I remained stoic, determined not to show any emotion. "I didn't send anything. My hands aren't on any of this."

Kingston took a step toward me. "I think you'll like this now." I glanced down at what he had in his hand, and I refused to fight the grin that appeared on my face. Kingston was one step ahead again. I took the object out of Kingston's hand and looked at Malcolm, who eyed the item in my hand.

"You think you've won."

"I don't think. I know."

"Shadow isn't going to stop until she's dead. He probably will kill you in the end too."

Ah, so this fucker has a name. "I have no problem taking him out, just like I'm about to do with you. In fact, I'll do it in a way that might seem familiar to you. Did you have Shadow kill Stewart with a knife like this one?"

I saw the fear enter his eyes for the first time since I stepped into the room. I watched as Malcolm's guards reached for their own guns, but before they could aim them, Kingston's men fired shots into their skulls. I couldn't help the adrenaline that was flying through my veins because I knew that it would have been all too easy to force the guards to give their guns up at the door. Kingston really didn't want them to see any of this coming and I couldn't help but smile about it.

The terror in Malcolm's eyes increased tenfold when his men fell to the ground like dominoes. I slowly walked behind him, never taking my eyes off him. I could see him shaking slightly in fear.

"But what about the deal we had? I signed the contract and if you kill me, it all will go up in smoke."

"Is this a last-ditch attempt at saving your life? Okay, I'll play for a second." I leaned down and whispered in his ear, "This stopped being about the money when you tried to take out what was mine. Now call off the hit."

I placed the knife up to his throat, yet he still said nothing. "Did you understand me? I said call off the hit."

"I can't."

"Why not?"

"Because I had a contingency plan that in case something like this happened, he would still carry out his mission. No matter what duress I was under, everything would go on as we'd planned."

Son of a bitch. "I want you to let me know how it feels as this knife pierces your skin." I pressed the knife deeper and smiled when a sliver of blood leaked from his throat. "What?

You don't have anything to say now? I haven't cut off your air supply yet or severed your jugular."

"I've said what I needed to say."

"Fine."

And then I put an end to it all.

I stepped to the side before handing Kingston the knife. "I need you to find everything on a hitman for hire named Shadow ASAP."

"Already on it."

27

GRACE

I looked up from the book I was reading as soon as I heard the lock on the front door unlatch. The excitement of having Broderick back was short-lived after I saw the look on his face. It was one I'd never seen before and after knowing him for over twenty years it frightened me. My brother's words rang in the back of my mind, and I knew it was about time to address everything that had been swirling through my head and the change in behavior that I saw from Broderick.

"What's wrong?"

He looked at me for the first time when he heard my voice. It was as if he hadn't known that I was in the room. "Why do you assume that something happened?"

"I've known you for too long not to."

"Fair enough," he said as he sat down next to me on the couch. I didn't know what I was waiting for him to say, but him not saying anything made things so much worse. The silence felt as if he were trying to break things down as nicely as possible, letting me down like a parent putting their infant to bed after they'd fallen asleep in their arms.

"Broderick, just spit it out."

"The person who hired a hitman to threaten you is dead."

I gasped as questions flooded my brain. "How'd he die? Is this all over?"

"The hitman still has orders to kill you and potentially me. And he's dead because I killed him."

"You did what?!"

That had been the last thing I thought he would say. I wasn't completely naive to how the Crosses sometimes did business but to go as far as to murder someone...

"I'm not happy about taking someone's life, but I did what I had to do to protect your life. The man Malcolm hired will get word that I killed Malcolm and that won't change his orders. He was already paid well in advance to make sure that you were dead."

"So he's just going to get more angry and continue coming after me until he kills me." Speaking of anger, I was growing more tense, wondering what this was going to turn into. I thought I had prepared myself for what could happen between us but now, more than anything, I felt as if things were spinning out of control.

"Over my dead body."

I took a deep breath, trying to calm myself down, and said, "So now what? Do we wait for him to strike again?"

"Kingston's men are looking for leads, but as of now we need to make sure he doesn't have a chance of getting to you."

I didn't say anything because I felt as if there should have been a *but* at the end of his statement. Just as I was calming down, he cleared his throat.

"That isn't the only thing I wanted to tell you."

The way he said it made my heart hurt.

"The person who broke into your home and left you that letter? It was organized by me."

"You paid someone to break into my house hoping that it would force me to move in with you?" I repeated what he said and wished that he would defend himself. When he said nothing, it confirmed my fear: Hunter was right. The calmness I was trying to achieve was long gone. My doubts and wonderment about how we'd make it past this turned into rage. "You are a fucking asshole."

Broderick's expression gave nothing away.

"So, you manipulated a situation in order to get me to do what you wanted me to do."

"Look, Grace, that isn't what—"

"That's exactly what happened! You deliberately played this situation so that it benefited you and got what you wanted. You must win by any means necessary. Not to mention that you killed him."

"Because he is trying to have you killed, don't you see that?" The distress in his voice was exacerbated and I could see the anger in his eyes.

"Broderick, what did killing him do?"

"Make it so that he never pulls this shit again."

"But it hasn't stopped the hitman from coming after me. You know how terrible I felt about Stewart and to then have you do the same thing I…" I couldn't find the words to finish my thought.

When he didn't even bother defending himself, I stood up and stormed out of the room, into the guest bedroom. I grabbed all of my things that were within reach and threw them into my bags. Some of the purchases I made while I was here, small things like body wash and shampoo, I left because I figured he could just throw them out if necessary.

"What are you doing?"

I stiffened at his question before I continued. "Exactly what you think I'm doing: packing to leave."

"You're not going anywhere."

I dropped the shirt into my bag before I turned to face him, rage coursing through me at five hundred miles per hour. "Or what? You're going to kill me too? Hire someone to cover up my murder much like you hired someone to scare me out of my home?"

My sarcastic question must have come out of left field for him because he didn't have an answer ready for me. I turned back around to continue packing before he finally said a word. "I killed him because he brought danger to your door, and I'd do it again in a heartbeat."

"Don't you see the disconnect here? I've made it my life's mission to help people and you have no problem just snatching life away."

"If he hadn't done what he did to you, he'd still be breathing the same air you and I are right now. I had a good reason to do what I did and I'm not ashamed of it."

I nodded, fighting back tears because I was determined for him not to see me cry. I grabbed a few more of my things, including my phone, which I called a car from before it landed in the back pocket of my jeans, and closed my bag. I'd never been more thankful to have packed light in my life.

I grabbed my bags and stared down at the man in front of me; the emotional rollercoaster I was on with him had been more than enough and I was ready to exit this ride. But would he let me go without a fight? One step was all I could take as I tested whether he would stand his ground or move out of the way. Another step didn't prove any different. My next step shoved me within six inches of him and I finally said, "Broderick, get out of my way."

Without a word, he moved and that was when I realized I was free. There was no need for me to flee under the shadow of night or try to hatch a plan that may or may not work. He was willing to let me go, which was what I wanted.

"Thank you," I whispered before I slipped past him and out of the guest room. I took one last look around the living room before I walked to the front door, determined not to look back and go crawling back to him.

When I made my way to the lobby of his building, I debated where I was going to go or what I was going to do. A few suggestions came to mind before I changed my destination on my phone. As soon as I put my phone back into its resting place, a car drove up and my heart thundered in my chest. The driver double-parked and rushed out of the car to, I assume, help me with my bags. Once we were both settled in the car, he looked at me in the rearview mirror and asked, "To the airport?"

I nodded. "To the airport."

28
GRACE

The power beneath my fingertips had a strange way of calming me down from the highs and lows I was experiencing. Every time I thought about what had transpired at Broderick's place, I became enraged, yet wept from the pain I was feeling. How had everything gone so wrong in such a short period of time?

I knew I was running from my problems and that it wasn't the correct answer. However, it was the one I needed at this time, and I was doing what was best for me.

I also knew that as soon as I ran, Broderick would still be keeping tabs on me due to him having Kingston's men watching my mother, so it wasn't as if I was completely out from under Broderick's thumb. Yet I felt freer.

I debated taking a flight to who knows where, but I ended up renting a car at the airport. It took a little more time because I didn't have a reservation, but it was well worth it now as I was on the open road, with no one around me. Whether Kingston's team knew I hadn't gotten on a plane or not I didn't know. Heck, maybe I was wrong and as soon as I stepped foot out of Broderick's home, he called them off.

My phone sat in the center console, begging me to check it, but I didn't want to read what might have been sent to me since I turned my phone off after arriving at the airport.

I pulled into the small driveway and sat there for a moment collecting my thoughts. The two story home that my mother purchased after she reevaluated where she wanted to live was as stunning now as it was when she purchased it and although it wasn't my childhood home, it still brought warm and fuzzy feelings due to the person who lived there.

I grabbed everything I packed and made my way to the front door. I smiled when Mom peeped through one of the side windows and she rushed to open the door.

"Hi, Mom."

Her eyes widened in shock as her mouth dropped open. "What a wonderful surprise! What are you doing here? Why does it look as if you've been crying?"

"Because I have been. It's a long story."

"Well, we have all night so why don't we get you settled in the guest room, and we can talk about it. Are you hungry? It would only take me a second to heat something up."

I nodded as my stomach growled. A home-cooked meal would be wonderful after the drive I'd just done. I didn't really want to speak about any of this with my mom, but maybe getting my feelings out there and talking to someone about them would help me feel better. "I'll get settled and take a quick shower if that's all right. Then I'll eat."

"Of course it is!" My mom smiled at me. "I'm just so happy that you're here." She rubbed her hand up and down my back before walking me to her guest room. It was much smaller than Broderick's, but that didn't mean I liked it any less. In fact, being here helped me feel more at ease with my decision to leave him. There was no way that I would have felt at peace in his home with the way things went down between us.

I washed away the doubts about whether I should have stayed as I showered. Broderick provided a safety net for me at his home from a killer who had no issue with attacking me, but it was almost as if being around Broderick and on his turf had become suffocating between him shutting down on me and then confessing what he did. No, I'd made the right choice in leaving, because it meant that I got to keep my sanity.

Once I was out of the shower and properly fed, I sat on the couch in my mother's living room and folded my legs underneath me. "There is no way I'm going to get out talking about this, huh?"

"Nope and I don't have classes tomorrow or the following day so we can stay up as long as we need to until you tell me everything that is going on."

I nodded as I took the long wet braid that I put my hair in after my shower and flipped it over my shoulder. I could only procrastinate for so long so it was time to confess everything.

I wasn't sure how long it took for me to get everything out, but I knew it all ended with tears streaming down my face and Mom pulling me into her arms, once again reassuring me that everything was going to be okay. We rocked back and forth slightly, the movement reminding me of how she would comfort me when I was a child, although my problems right now were much bigger than any I'd faced back then.

"We need to talk about you having people watch me, but that can be saved for later. This hurts more because you're in love with him. And he loves you. Selena and I noticed this when you two were younger but didn't want to interfere."

She said it so matter-of-factly, not leaving any room for me to deny it. Plus, I wouldn't because she was right at least about my feelings.

I pulled away and wiped my eyes with my hands. "Yes. I could have moved past the murder, although it's not necessarily something I agree with, but the manipulation hurts." His feelings for me weren't something I wanted to talk about right now.

Mom leaned over and grabbed a tissue off the end table and handed it to me. "Yeah, he was a complete shit for doing that."

I giggled before I could cover my mouth. "Since when do you cuss?"

She shrugged. "I'm turning over a new leaf, I guess. Do you miss him?"

"I do. Don't know if I'll ever make it past what he's done though. This is a huge deal."

"And you're worried about forgiving him too easily."

I nodded. "It's a mixture of that and me being genuinely hurt about this. The hours it took to get up here gave me a lot of time to think and just be by myself and I didn't realize how much I was holding in. I know that part of the reason he did it was to, yes, have me closer to him but it was his way of protecting me."

"So he had good intentions at least for part of it."

"Yes, he just used manipulation as a tactic to get me to do what he wanted."

"You don't need to decide about that now. Take some time

to think about it and then make a decision. Have you heard from him since you left?"

"I'm not sure. I've had my phone on silent the entire time."

"Well? Doesn't hurt to see if there are any signs that he cares about you as much as I think he does. I bet he reached out to you."

I walked over to my coat and pulled my phone out. "How do you know this?"

"I've known Broderick since he was a child. He wouldn't go through all of this hassle for someone he didn't care about. You could probably get Selena to confirm if you really wanted to."

I shook my head as I powered up my phone's screen. Just like my mother said, I had messages from Broderick.

Broderick: *I know I'm the last person that you probably want to talk to, but I needed to say this. I shouldn't have sent that message and for that I'm deeply sorry.*

Broderick: *You should have had the right to choose what you wanted to do, and I shouldn't have forced your hand.*

Broderick: *Let me know that you're okay.*

I debated texting him back for a moment before I did so.

Me: *I'm fine. Thanks for checking in.*

A knock on the door startled us. Who would be knocking at this time of night? I held my phone in my hand as I walked to the door, my mother trailing close behind me. "Who is it?"

"Nick, I work for Cross Sentinel."

"How do I know that you're telling the truth?"

"I'm happy to call Kingston to confirm."

I looked over at my mother, who was already typing on

her phone. "I'm sending a message to Selena to send us Kingston's number," she whispered.

"Good thinking," I whispered back. "Give us just a moment," I shouted back at the door.

"Take your time."

When we had Kingston's number in hand, I quickly called him and confirmed that Nick had been watching my mother. Once we verified his identity, we opened the door with Kingston on the phone, who said, "I wanted Nick to introduce himself. If you all need anything, he'll be there to help."

"So I guess we should tell you that we have plans on going shopping tomorrow?" I asked.

My mom looked at me from the corner of her eye. "We do?"

"Yes, it's something you've wanted to do so we're doing that as long as Nick and Kingston deem it safe. I don't want to risk anyone else's life."

Kingston spoke up for the two men. "Nothing Nick has reported to me says differently. I just want him to stay closer to you than he has been doing."

I wrapped my arm around Mom and smiled. "That works for me."

Finally, I could do something more normal again, something that I knew would burn off some of the stress I felt.

29

BRODERICK

I felt like shit. There was no other way for me to put it. It wasn't even a physical pain, but more of an emotional ache that I'd never felt before.

I continued working from home, which was the only thing that felt normal. I'd gone from living on my own to wanting another person to be with me no matter the cost. I'd grown used to looking forward to seeing Grace's face after I'd finished work and even thought about what life might be like with her once things returned to normal and she went back to work. Yet here I was, sitting here in my apartment all alone.

I sent her several messages a couple of hours ago, but they went undelivered, convincing me that her phone was off. It took everything in me not to storm the city to find out where she'd gone. The only hint I had was that she went to the airport but didn't board a flight.

The only person who knew for sure that she was gone was Kingston because I wanted his team to be on the lookout for when she resurfaced. Or so I thought. The knock on the door told me that that thought might have been false, since I wasn't expecting anyone to come over.

I debated whether to answer it, but it seemed as if I was going to be forced to be social since I heard the front door open. Damn me for giving both of my brothers a key to my apartment. Kingston had one too, but I figured he would have at least called before arriving. My siblings were more brash in their decision-making at times.

"You look like shit." Of course it was my twin who spoke first.

"Glad I look as good as I feel."

Damien looked at Gage and said, "Looks like Kingston was right."

Kingston was a traitor. "So you both know everything so I don't need to go into the details of what happened. Excellent."

"Why didn't you come to one of us before you hired someone to plant a note in her home?"

"I wasn't thinking straight. It was as if my brain was scrambled, and I needed to get her in my home to protect her by any means necessary."

"Love. Love made you do it."

I raised an eyebrow at Damien before Gage took a step forward. He looked me dead in the eye and it had been a while since I'd seen this look in his eye. It told me that he knew something I hadn't been willing to admit. "You love her."

Bingo.

It wasn't worth hiding it anymore. "I do. Have for a long time now and didn't realize it. All of that is probably up in smoke now given the stupid thing that I did, but I can admit out loud now that I love her."

Damien grinned. "Welcome to the other side, brother."

Gage groaned. "Another one down."

I rolled my eyes. "It isn't the worst thing in the world. You should probably try it sometime."

"I'm good. Trust me."

The buzzing of my phone prevented me from answering and when I read the text message, I sighed with relief.

Kingston: *She's in Brentson with her mother. She's fine.*

Me: *Perfect. Anything new on Shadow?*

Kingston: *Nothing. No signs of him still being in New York City. Don't worry though we have eyes on your girl.*

I smiled just before I heard Damien ask, "What happened?"

"Kingston just said that she arrived at her mother's home in Brentson. Unharmed. She's safe."

"How does he know that?" Gage asked.

"Grace and I agreed to have some of Cross Sentinel watch her family just in case Shadow tried to take one of them out because of their connection to us. We didn't tell her family just in case them knowing what was going on would make them bigger targets, instead choosing to have them have a 'guardian angel' of sorts that stood in the wings."

"Some would consider that a violation of privacy."

I wasn't about to get into it with Gage right now. "I viewed it as the best option that we had at the time and Grace agreed. So we did it. And just because she left doesn't mean that I was going to take that protection away from them."

Damien put his hand on my shoulder and squeezed. "So

you know all of that lovey-dovey stuff that you just spewed to us? Why don't you show her that?"

I was thankful for the change in conversation, however slight. "You know what? You're right. I'm going to give her a couple of days alone with her mother and then I'm going up there to tell her."

"Ric, this might be the first good plan you've had in ages. Well, outside of killing Malcolm."

"So help me if you call Ric one more time..."

The smile on Gage's face said that, once again, he was doing it to get a rise out of me. His eyes looked brighter, and I wondered if whatever he had been working on was complete. But right now wasn't the time to ask.

"Brentson, we haven't been back there in years."

I nodded. "It's going to be weird being back there after all of this time."

Brentson University was where all three of us had gone to college. A prestigious school that was held in high regard by many, it had instilled in us a wonderful education that helped us lay the foundation for us to take on our roles in Cross Industries as well as make our own marks with our own businesses. Brentson was a cute college town, and I was sure returning would bring many memories, although my focus was getting the one person who meant everything to me back.

I spent some time with my brothers and once they left, I started concocting a plan about how I was going to bring Grace back where she belongs: with me.

My phone rang just as I was about to head into the living room and the name that appeared on my screen gave me pause. I knew I needed to take this call to salvage any part of this relationship, so I answered the phone.

"Hunter."

"I'm surprised you answered the phone."

"Me too."

Hunter laughed briefly, easing some of the tension that was being volleyed back and forth as soon as I answered the phone.

Before he could say anything else, I spoke. "Look, I should have been more upfront about my feelings for your sister."

"Yes, you should have. Especially after the discussion we had years ago. In terms of relationships, I didn't trust you as far as I could throw you."

"Understandable." There was nothing to defend there. He'd known me for way too long and knew about my transgressions in the past.

"That being said, if you make her happy and treat her right, then that's what matters here. She can make her own decisions and if she chose you, that makes me happy."

"So we're good?"

He sighed. "We're good. And I also trust you to get this asshole who seems to be after my sister."

"Yes. We have some leads we're following and hopefully will track him down soon."

"Good. Is she around? Thought I could just chat with her for a moment."

I was hoping he wouldn't ask this. "She's not here." I could have said that in a better way. Having all of this uncertainty was throwing me off my game.

Hunter paused. "Where is she?" His words were

measured and slow, almost making me wonder if the progress we'd just made was for naught.

"She's visiting your mother, but Kingston's team is up there guarding them." I decided keeping the entire story about what happened between us quiet was wise in the instance.

"And you didn't go with her?"

I chose my words carefully this time. "She wanted some time to herself, and I respected her wishes."

"Well, I'll reach out to Mom and her. I'll talk to you later."

"Okay."

"Broderick?" He said my name just before I had the opportunity to hang up.

"Yes?"

"Break her heart and she won't be the only person you'll have to worry about coming after you. I don't give a shit how much money you have."

I bit back a chuckle. The only person who could ruin me was Grace. "Understood."

I hung up the phone and walked into my living room, where I left my computer on the coffee table. When I sat down on my couch, laptop in hand, I heard my phone vibrate on the coffee table. I grabbed it, anticipating a message from Kingston.

Grace: *I'm fine. Thanks for checking in.*

I longed to reply to her or to call her on the phone, but I held back. She needed and wanted space, and I was going to give it to her. Once that was over, it was game on.

30

GRACE

The next morning, I woke up and stretched, happy to see the new day, yet dreading what was to come. Taking some time to myself last night had given me some time to assess the situation and gave me some room to breathe. Was I still angry that Broderick manipulated the situation to convince me to stay with him? Yes. But my anger had lessened overnight, and I had to admit to myself that I missed being with him.

I got out of bed and stretched again before I heard something. I could hear voices outside of my room, but I assumed that Mom had just turned on the television while drinking her coffee. I wasn't prepared for the scene that unfolded in front of me when I opened the door.

"Dad?"

"Good morning, sweetheart."

I looked at my mother, who was sitting across from him at her dining room table and raised an eyebrow. "I didn't know he was stopping by either. What a lovely surprise right?"

They seemed to be getting along quite well, which

shocked me. The last time I saw them in a room together, it ended with my mother taking every bit of her energy to scream at him to leave her alone.

"What are you doing here?" I crossed my arms over my chest, preparing myself for battle. Although my mother seemed to be at peace with him being here, I couldn't say that I was.

"I come to visit your mother almost every weekend. Has been happening for months."

I looked over at Mom to confirm and she did.

"Things are better between us, kiddo, and I wanted to make amends with both you and Hunter."

The sound that left my throat wasn't human. I didn't need this right now. "You? Are you trying to make amends after leaving our mother during what I can assume was one of the worst moments of her life? She was fighting cancer for crying out loud! You left her to fight it alone while Hunter and I tried to pick up the pieces. I don't think you understand the gravity of the situation here."

"This is why I've been trying to reach out."

I sighed and ran a hand through the waves that my hair ended up in after I'd taken out my braid. "I wasn't ready to talk to you then and I'm for damn sure not ready now. I'll hang out in the guest room until you leave." I looked over at my mother and asked, "Are we still going shopping in Brentson?"

With a sad smile, she nodded and said, "Yes, of course. Sometime this afternoon."

I turned on my heel and left. Once I was safely behind the door of the guest room, I sighed before crawling back into bed and reaching over to grab my phone.

Hunter: *Is everything alright? Heard you were visiting Mom.*

Disappointed was an understatement as deep down, I somewhat hoped that Broderick would reach out again, even though I didn't know what I would say back to him. However, it was clear that Hunter had spoken to him. Instead of sending Broderick a text message, though the temptation was there, I replied to my brother.

Me: *Hey Hunter, I'm hanging out with Mom for a little while I still have some time off.*

He didn't respond right away, but someone else texted me instead.

Unknown Number: *Hey this is Anais. Damien told me about what happened, and I wanted to reach out to see if you were okay.*

I smiled, happy to have someone to talk to about it all.

Me: *I'm about as good as could be expected, I guess. Thanks for asking.*

Our conversation continued as I waited for my parents' visit to end.

When there was a knock on my door about an hour later, I wished I could say I was surprised to find that when I opened it my father was standing on the other side, but I wasn't. The brief time apart had given me an opportunity to not only pull myself together, but mentally prepare for this moment I knew he would take. My father hadn't gotten to where he was in the business world without his instincts.

I moved aside to let him walk past me and when he sat down on a chair in the bedroom, I sat down at the foot of the bed, hoping to still maintain some distance between us.

"I'm just going to cut to the chase. Grace, I'm sorry. Sorry for letting your mother down, as well as you and your brother. Seeing your mother in such a state screwed me up. I made sure she was well taken care of but mentally I wasn't there. I failed."

I nodded. "I'm not going to disagree with that. Hunter and I took on a lot to make sure all of Mom's affairs were in order, no matter which way things turned out. And you weren't there. You essentially abandoned us a couple of years ago and didn't look back."

"I kept up with her prognosis and how her treatments were going. I kept in constant contact with her too."

I glared at him and folded my arms across my chest. "So you had no issues with Hunter and I struggling while we watched our mother go through the hardest fight of her life."

Dad looked at me for the first time since he'd knocked on the door. Tears were flowing from his eyes, and he did nothing to stop them. This might have been the first time I'd seen him in this state. "I have no excuses. And I know that nothing I say will fix the damage I've caused. The only thing I can say is that I'm sorry. My mind couldn't bear to see the woman that I've loved all of these years going through this and I could only wish that in time, you'll forgive me."

He stood up and rubbed his hands along his pants. "I love your mother and both you and your brother so much. I'm going to head out, but if you ever want to talk about... anything, you have my number."

I nodded as I watched my father leave, closing the door quietly behind him.

∼

"I NEED to come up here more often."

"That's what I've been telling you. Isn't this town

perfect? Not to mention the company you're keeping," Mom said jokingly as we walked down the street. We spent the better part of the afternoon shopping in Brentson, and it felt wonderful to spend some time together again. Even if it meant having a bodyguard following close behind.

I chuckled because it was true. She'd been telling me to come visit her more and I'd always been so busy living my life in New York City, but I couldn't deny that the change of pace, even under these circumstances, felt great. Spending this time with my mother was precious and something that I so desperately needed. Plus, we'd had our own personal chauffeur in Nick. We didn't want to risk not knowing what Shadow might have done to my rental car during the night and Nick's car was safer.

Once we were all settled into the back seat Nick pulled out of the parking spot and soon we were on our way back to my mother's house. She lived outside of Brentson in a cozy cottage not too far from the university, just enough to feel as if she was outside of the small college town.

Few people were on the road as we cruised along the mostly empty streets. That didn't last for long, however. I heard a motor rev in the background and Nick's eyes darted to the rearview mirror. I turned my head to look through the back windshield and saw that a motorcycle was gaining on us quickly.

"Hold on and duck down!" Nick shouted and I quickly did, bringing my mother down with me. He accelerated and I felt my mother grab my hand for dear life. I watched out of the corner of my eye as Nick maneuvered the vehicle and clicked a button.

"I'm calling in an attack on my vehicle heading west away from Brentson, New York. Motorcycle is gaining on me."

My mom screamed when the first gunshot hit the back window.

"We're going to make it through this." The words tumbled out of my mouth quickly, but she understood me because she gave another squeeze.

"Is everyone okay?"

"Yes!" I said and I quietly hoped that this wasn't the end. The answer I received was the sound of more gunshots hitting the car.

"The car is bulletproof, but I don't want to take any chances."

I could understand that, but what made things more troubling was that I could hear the roar of the motorcycle getting closer, as if he were chasing us down. Yet panic hadn't gripped a hold of my heart yet. If the car was bulletproof like Nick said, I assumed his fear wasn't necessarily of us getting shot, but the motorcycle driver being able to get close enough to run us off the road and then make his move.

My mother glanced up and screamed again. I turned to look and found the motorcycle near my door.

I felt the car jerk to the left, the side I was sitting on, and I assumed Nick was trying to run the motorcycle off the road. Instead, the motorcyclist held up a gun and aimed it directly for Nick. Before I heard another gunshot however, I heard the squealing of tires and the motorcyclist disappeared.

I looked back over at Nick and could see that he was gripping the wheel for dear life. He yanked the steering wheel again and I could hear tires screech as I pleaded in my head for us to make it out of this alive. He pulled to a stop about a minute or two later.

"What are you doing?"

Nick looked at me before opening the door. "Everything is fine now."

"How do you know that?"

Instead of answering me, he exited the vehicle, but he didn't go far. He was standing next to my door, and I sat up and banged on it.

When he didn't respond, I looked over at my mom who was just staring at me in shock.

"Are you okay?"

All she could do was nod. When I heard my door open, I looked up at Nick ready to tell him that he'd lost his mind, but it wasn't Nick standing there.

31

BRODERICK

The power of this Ferrari was something else. I could have taken another one of the cars I owned to Brentson, but this felt right. I didn't drive the Ferrari that Gage had gifted me often, preferring my SUVs or to hire a car while in the city, but being out on this open road was nice even if I couldn't fully exercise how fast this car could go.

It was a lovely afternoon and the perfect day to get the woman I loved back.

It felt so damn good to say that.

I was only a couple of miles outside of Brentson when my phone rang. The Bluetooth in the car picked it up and showed that it was Kingston calling.

"What's up, man?"

"Where are you?"

The seriousness in his voice made me grab the steering wheel tighter. "On my way to Brentson. Why?"

"Good. Shadow found Grace and—"

Red. All I saw was red. The son of a bitch found them.

Before he could tell me more information, my foot added pressure to the gas. Thoughts of not breaking the law left my mind as the only thing that circled my thoughts was getting to Grace. "Where are they?"

"State Street. On their way back from town to head to her mother's. Nick is driving one of our bulletproof vehicles. Shadow's on a motorcycle. We have other teams racing into town as well, but it'll take them some time to get there."

"I'm only a couple of miles out so I'll probably get there first." A sign that said welcome to Brentson greeted me as I flew into town.

"I was hoping you'd say that."

Instinct kicked in as I remembered the roads that I used to travel on while attending school here. I swung a left down another street hoping this would still lead me to State Street quicker. When my GPS gawked about giving me new directions, I shut it off. I hoped my gut was right.

"Is Grace's father still in town?" Kingston told me that Lewis had traveled up to visit Jill early this morning when he briefed me as I was wrapping up a few things before I left.

"He is as far as I know."

"Yes..." I mumbled as the road I thought would lead to State Street did. "Okay, I'm going to call him quickly and have him meet me. Hopefully he can connect with Hunter as well because I won't have time to do that."

"Sounds good."

"Let me know if you hear anything else." I hung up without waiting for an answer. State Street was empty for this time of day and that made me happy. I hoped that a police officer wouldn't try to pull me over as I pressed harder down on the gas determined to get to my woman by any means necessary.

"Call Lewis McCartney," I said, commanding my in-car navigation to do so.

"Calling Lewis McCartney."

While the call was connecting, I popped open the center console where I stored my pistol just before I left New York City. I usually kept it in a safe in my cars, but something told me to put it within reach and I was glad I did.

Finally, Lewis picked up. "Broderick, to what do I owe this call to?"

"Get to State Street as soon as possible. Don't stop driving until you see several cars and a motorcycle."

"What are—"

"Don't question me. Get down here right now."

I hung up the phone, not giving him anytime to come to terms with what I'd just said. I could see a motorcycle in the distance, and I knew it was going to be now or never. I floored it and could see the sedan that the motorcycle was chasing. The motorcycle was fast, but I was faster and quickly gaining on him.

The only thing I could hear was the ferocious roar of the car that I controlled as my mind zeroed in on protecting Grace. I watched as Shadow shot at the vehicle that I assumed held Grace and her mother and it only enraged me further. I couldn't wait to get my hands on this hitman and show him that he didn't mess with what was mine.

As if he knew that someone was closing in on him, I watched as Shadow looked over his shoulder and in a split instance, I jerked the wheel and sure enough, he began firing shots at me. I didn't have a bulletproof car, but what I did have was the ability to shoot. This needed to end not only to save everyone in the car up ahead's lives, but the lives of anyone who might be in the surrounding area, and this car chase could end up injuring or killing many people.

When Shadow drove around the car and was next to the back door of the car Grace was in, I took the shot. The bullet appeared to hit Shadow somewhere in the back and was enough to get him away from the sedan. When I saw that he swerved and almost crashed his motorcycle into the ground, I smiled and stopped my car once I was a few feet ahead of him, essentially putting the Ferrari in between the motorcycle and the sedan. He would have to go through me literally if he wanted to get anywhere near Grace.

I parked my car and walked toward him, rage guiding me every step of the way.

He was lying on the ground looking up at the sky with a weird smile on his face when I approached him. His gun was a few inches away from his hand and I kicked it even further away when I walked up to it.

"It's good to see you, Broderick."

The familiarity he had with my name didn't sit well with me. "Can't say the same about you. Any last words before I put a permanent end to this?" I aimed my gun at his forehead.

"No." The smile grew wider. "Well, there is one."

His pause was meant for entertainment value that I had no intention of appreciating.

"You're in for a rude awakening."

I raised an eyebrow at him and when he tried to reach for his gun again, I shot him, not caring that he hadn't given me any more information. The immediate threat to Grace's life was gone. I knew that although the temptation was there, Grace wouldn't want to save this asshole.

When I let the bullet fly through his head, a sense of satisfaction passed through me. I was willing to bet that Damien felt similarly when he shot Carter for kidnapping Anais.

After I made sure that he was dead, I turned around and saw dark vehicles racing toward us. My first instinct was that the cops were on their way, but not hearing any sirens told me that it was Cross Sentinel instead.

Not bothering to wait to find out because I had better things to do, I walked toward the sedan that had been the center of all of this. Nick exited the car and nodded at me. I nodded back as we silently communicated thanks to one another and when he opened the back door, I couldn't help but smile in relief that Grace looked to be okay and unharmed. That was when my soul was allowed to breathe.

32

GRACE

"Broderick?!"

Seeing Broderick standing there almost made me weep. I quickly undid my seat belt and jumped out of the car and into his arms. I was shaking like a leaf as he pulled me closer into his embrace. I didn't know how much I'd been shaken up by the ordeal until he pulled closer to him. Oh, how I'd missed him. If there were any traces of anger left, they were long gone now.

"Don't cry. You don't have to worry about Shadow anymore and Cross Sentinel is here to clear everything up. Look."

I followed where Broderick's hand was pointing. The same shocked look that I found on my mother's face could be found on mine. There was the motorcycle that I had seen out of my window lying a few feet away from a body with a lot of other people surrounding it. A sports car was parked between the body and our car.

"Is he dead?"

Broderick nodded. "I made sure of it, and I won't apologize for that. I did it out of love."

"I don't want you to," I said before pulling his head down so that his lips could meet my own, but I froze. "You what?"

"I love you. With every fiber of my being. Wholeheartedly. With everything—"

I stopped his speech with a kiss that had been a long time coming. When we broke apart, I said, "I love you too."

"If you ever want to stop me from talking, feel free to do that anytime."

I smiled, feeling a sense of relief for the first time in a very long time. I looked to my right and found my mom standing next to us.

"Someone has a lot of explaining to do," she said as she eyed Broderick.

"I can help with that, Dr. McCartney."

I smiled. I wasn't the only person who had the letters "D.R." in front of my name.

"Jill!"

We turned once more and saw my father jogging up to us. I briefly looked around him and found his car parked on the other side of the street from where we were. When he reached us, he immediately pulled my mother into his arms, grabbing her as if he loosened even a tiny bit, that she would vanish.

"Broderick called me when he was closing in on your location. Are you all right?" He looked at me too but seemed more hesitant to approach me. "Are you both okay?"

My mother nodded and he pulled her in for another hug. The way she saw comfort in my father once again forced me to reconsider whether it was worth keeping this grudge against him.

A squeeze of my shoulder drew my eyes up to Broderick and the slight dip of his head before he looked at my parents showed me that he had an idea about what I was thinking about. He leaned down and whispered in my ear, "They're happy again."

"I know."

"And you deserve to be too."

～

My shirt was off before we reached the door. The remote cabin that Broderick had rented just outside of Brentson was the perfect quick getaway to do just this: fuck each other's brains out.

Broderick finally opened the door and once we were both inside, he slammed the door shut and turned around and backed me into it. Soon, his lips were on mine once again doing everything he could to make me go wild.

It was the first time we'd been alone in days, and we were making up for lost time. I knew that at least this first time was going to be quick. But any other thoughts that I might have had left my mind when Broderick stopped kissing me long enough to remove my pants.

I thought he would stand up and take my lips again, but he turned his focus to my pussy. He threw one of my legs over his shoulder and feasted on me. I closed my eyes and let my hands roam through his short brown hair as I enjoyed the way he was making me feel all the while trying to maintain my balance so that he could continue ravishing me. My head fell back as he switched from using his mouth on me to using his fingers to drive pleasure through my body. As the orgasm ripped through my body, I briefly opened my eyes and watched him finish his job.

When he gave me a moment to catch my breath, I said, "I want your cock in my mouth."

Broderick shook his head. "Not enough time," he said before he turned me around and entered me from behind while my body was pressed up against the door.

"Broderick," I moaned as I embraced the feeling of his cock inside of me. His name on my lips only encouraged him further as he pumped in and out of me.

"This is going to be quick." His voice quivered as if he was barely hanging on.

"Don't worry I had the same thought. I'm already close."

"Well then, let's bring it home."

Broderick's thrusts grew more powerful as I turned to look over my shoulder. Suddenly he stopped and pulled out of me. He turned me around.

"What—"

"I want to watch your face as I fuck you," he said before picking me up and placing me on the dining room table in the cabin. There, he pushed his dick inside me once more and his stare remained on me as we watched each other as I grew closer to my second orgasm, When the feeling overtook me, I gasped out loud and Broderick leaned forward and kissed me, stopping any noise from leaving my mouth. A few more thrusts led to his release and both of us being out of breath.

Neither one of us dared to move, only taking the time to

catch our breaths. After a few moments we both got cleaned up and crawled into the lone bed in the cabin.

"I think my shirt might still be outside."

"What can I say? It was in the way of getting what I wanted: you naked."

I swung my blonde hair over my shoulder. "Lucky for you, that's what I wanted to be as well."

Broderick chuckled at my assertion. His joy was contagious as I felt myself smiling before he took a step forward. In response, I backed up into the room and when he continued to advance, I soon found myself with my body standing against the bed. Based on the predatory look in his eyes, I knew it was only a matter of time before I'd end up on my back with him hovering over me.

But we had plenty of time for that.

It was a couple days after the events unfolded and things were quieting down. Broderick offered to let us have a staycation of sorts so that we both could relax. After all, I needed to go back to work soon, and I was looking forward to it.

He lifted my head up so that my eyes met his. "You know that I'm proud of you."

"Why's that?"

"You've done so many things over the course of the last several days that I wouldn't have expected anyone to do. Your life has been in turmoil for weeks and you didn't crumble."

I slowly nodded my head. "You're right, but you know what makes it weirder?"

"What's that?"

I composed my thoughts for a second. "Malcolm's decision to make sure that there were no loose ends in case Dennis told me anything? Was all for naught. He didn't say a word because he was unconscious the moment he arrived at my hospital."

Broderick said nothing, and I couldn't read his expression. "What are you thinking about?"

"Your observation. I don't know what to think of it."

"That makes both of us, but there is another thing I wanted to mention."

"What's that?"

"I can't believe you gave me the space I needed." I played with the hair on his chest, loving the way it felt between my fingers.

"You don't know how hard that was."

A smirk appeared on my face. "I want to make a terrible joke right now and I—"

"Don't. Don't ruin the moment but yes, I only lasted less than two days without you. I could have gone about keeping you safe differently and for that I apologize, but I will never apologize for doing my best to protect you."

I chuckled. "I know. And if you hadn't come up here today, I probably would have called and asked for you to come up here immediately. I missed you way too much."

"Same goes both ways. I meant what I said earlier. I love you."

"And I love you."

EPILOGUE
BRODERICK

"So what is this meeting all about?" I asked as I got comfortable on my couch. I didn't want to be on this call because I had other more important things to be doing, particularly the woman who was standing in the kitchen pouring two glasses of wine for us right now. Things were going well between us and with everyone in our lives. It seemed as if things were finally settling down.

"Damn if I know," Damien responded. "Maybe it's Kingston going to confess that the reason why he drops by my apartment building more often than not to make sure that everything is okay is because he's hoping to catch a glimpse of Ellie."

I choked back a laugh and as Kingston was about to respond when Dad spoke up. "Can I make an announcement first?"

"Sure, Uncle Martin."

Dad cleared his throat. "We have a bit of a personnel change. Since Gage cannot keep an assistant for longer than five seconds nowadays, we are going to shift things a bit.

Melissa will be Gage's new assistant while Isabelle will be Damien's. Let's see how that situation works out."

"Dad if you run off Melissa due to this, I'll—"

Dad interrupted Damien. "I think she can handle this."

Gage made a motion to respond before Kingston cut him off. "I really have something important to discuss. We need to talk about the hit that was put out on Grace."

My eyes darted over to Grace, who heard the question that had just come from my speakers. I was taking a short meeting with my brothers, Kingston, and my father although I was supposed to be enjoying the first evening that Grace and I had with one another in a while since she'd returned to work and I to my busy schedule. I hadn't been expecting Kingston's comment and it was clear that no one else in the virtual meeting had been either. I focused back on the screen.

"Malcolm lied; he didn't put the hit out on Grace. He knew who put the hit out though."

"Wait, what? How do you know this?"

This time, Kingston spoke up. "We got this video sent to us today. Confirmed its authenticity. Let me share my screen."

"Broderick, you think that you've won," Malcolm said before a sickly smile appeared on his face. I was reminded that he uttered the same words before I slit his throat. "But this is far from over."

"See, I'm not the one who put a hit out on your girlfriend, but you should be anxious about who did. Because they are still out there, watching your every move. And I'm not just talking about you. I'm talking about your entire family."

"You all fucked with the wrong person and now it's time to pay the price." The video ended abruptly after that.

"Remember that we thought that someone else had to be

funding Vincent in his endeavor to get revenge on Dad and to hurt Damien?"

"Yes, of course."

"This lines up with what Malcolm just said. There's someone else pulling the puppet strings who we know nothing about."

Dad cleared his throat. "This means that for now on, everyone on this call shouldn't take their security measures for granted. Who knows when or how this person will strike next."

∼

THANK you for reading Shadow Empire! While Grace and Broderick's story is complete, the Broken Cross series continues with Secret Empire, Gage and Melissa's book. Keep reading to find a sneak peek of it!

DON'T WANT to let Broderick and Grace go just yet? Click HERE to grab a bonus scene featuring the couple!

WANT to join discussions about the Broken Cross Series? Click HERE to join my Reader Group on Facebook.

PLEASE JOIN my newsletter to find out the latest about the Broken Cross series and my other books!

SECRET EMPIRE BLURB

Forbidden moments and secrets...

She ran and hid in one of the biggest cities in the world.

It's the best place to remain anonymous if you try hard enough.

But that all comes crashing down when I spend the night with her.

My new assistant.

I made a vow to never mention the night we spent together again.

She didn't know who I was and I preferred to keep it that way.

But when her past comes back to haunt her

I'm the only one who can help her fight the demons that curse her.

SNEAK PEEK AT SECRET EMPIRE
MELISSA

I'd just had the best sex of my life and I don't even know his name.

This wasn't something I usually practiced, since coming to New York City, but I couldn't deny the thrill that it gave me.

I closed my door with a resounding thud, but my thoughts refused to waiver from what had just occurred.

I walked into my bathroom and ripped the mask off my face. I thought about taking it off in the taxi on the way home, but I didn't want the driver to sense what had happened. When I looked at myself in the mirror, my face was lit up as bright as a spotlight and the redness in it did nothing for my complexion. If the definition of having fantastic sex was written in the dictionary, my picture would be listed right next to it. As I stared at myself, all I could hear was the low rumble of his voice in my ear.

Sweetheart.

I could take that nickname in many ways but hearing the name flow off his lips was an aphrodisiac. The way he said it sounded as if he owned my whole body and soul although it was just for that moment. Hell, I could surrender to him right now if he was here and I heard him whisper it to me.

Tonight took away the pain for a short period of time.

Shifting my attention, I turned on the shower, determined to remove tonight's events from my skin. I glanced up at the shower head as the water beat down over me, thankful to be able to afford this living space. If Damien Cross hadn't hired me, I don't know where I would be right now.

You know exactly where you'd be.

My inner thoughts confessed the truth, one that I couldn't deny if I tried.

Once I pulled my hair up, hoping to avoid getting it wet, I stepped foot into the shower with a sigh, allowing the water to flow around my body. I repeated a mantra that got me through the hard times.

I'm not going back there.

Most times it helped, but tonight was something different. A slight shiver ran down my spine, but I wasn't cold. My shower was ruined because of the memories that continued to haunt me.

I wrapped up my shower and exited much quicker than I intended. When I was out of the bathroom, I double-checked the locks on my door and windows to be safe. Once that was done, I walked into the kitchen and snatched my phone off of the countertop before leaning back on it. Although I tried to keep work at work, sometimes staying busy was helpful to keep me from tumbling into thoughts of my past. Or I could spend my time thinking about the adventure that my body had been taken on tonight.

That would have been lovely, except I knew I would never see that person again. But damn if I didn't still hear his voice in my head. I knew he was talking in more hushed tones due to where we were and the event we were attending, but his words still had their intended effect.

I closed my eyes briefly before concentrating on my phone, I checked my work email to see if there was anything pressing to attend to. When I found an email from Martin Cross in my inbox, I nearly threw my phone across the room. With a shaky thumb, I opened it.

Subject: *New Assignment*

Hi Melissa,

I've asked my assistant to send you a calendar invite to come and meet with me and Damien on Monday morning. We want to discuss with you a change in your role with the company.

Sincerely,

Martin

What the hell? My thoughts raced at what this could mean. At least it didn't sound as if I was losing my job. That was something I couldn't afford to do, nor did I truly want it. Working for Cross Industries had been mostly a dream. Every job had its ups and downs but for the most part, my time in this position had been lovely. Plus, I was grateful to Damien and Martin for taking a chance on me, having been young when I applied for the job.

Maybe it was a promotion? That would be wonderful.

Another email came through just as I was closing out of the one from Martin and without a second thought, I opened it. What I saw made me almost drop my phone on the ground. I had vowed never to open an email from that person again, but I couldn't predict the future. I couldn't believe they'd found me.

∾

Secret Empire is available now!

ABOUT THE AUTHOR

Bri loves a good romance, especially ones that involve a hot anti-hero. That is why she likes to turn the dial up a notch with her own writing. Her Broken Cross series is her debut dark romance series.

She spends most of her time hanging out with her family, plotting her next novel, or reading books by other romance authors.

briblackwood.com

ALSO BY BRI BLACKWOOD

Broken Cross Series

Sinners Empire (Prequel)

Savage Empire

Scarred Empire

Steel Empire

Shadow Empire

Secret Empire

Stolen Empire

Brentson University Series

Devious Game

Made in United States
Cleveland, OH
30 December 2024